ANVI

A BLESSING TO A CURSE

PARTH DUBEY

Contents

About The Author

Parth Dubey, the author of "Anvi: A Blessing to a Curse," is a poet and novelist born and raised in India. Drawing inspiration from the diverse people around him, Parth is a traveler at heart, having covered thousands of kilometers on his motorcycle, gathering stories from every corner.

"Anvi" is his second self-published work, following the success of "Kathan: An Epitaph to Be Buried." Parth sees his life as a blessing, and his destiny is to explore the world and narrate the tales he encounters. With each word, he unravels the intricate threads of human experience, inviting readers to join him on a literary journey of self-discovery.

Foreword

In the enchanting pages of "Anvi," Parth leads readers on a poignant journey through the intricate tapestry of a young girl's life, woven with the threads of love, rebellion, and self-discovery. The novel depicts the protagonist's troubles as she battles the weight of familial expectations.

As we delve into the story, we are introduced to Anvi, a spirited soul yearning for answers from her strict and proud father. The interplay between Anvi and her father forms the heart of this tale, exploring the delicate balance between obedience and the pursuit of one's own truth.

Anvi's journey is not just a quest for answers but a profound exploration of identity, autonomy, and the innate desire to chart one's own course. Her character, richly developed and relatable, invites readers to reflect on their own struggles, aspirations, and the universal pursuit of meaning.

The author skillfully navigates the emotional terrain of Anvi's life, weaving a narrative that resonates with authenticity and depth. Through the highs and lows, readers will find themselves drawn into a world where familial bonds are tested, personal convictions are forged, and the human spirit rises above adversity.

Preface

As I pen down the preface for "Anvi," I am reminded of the delicate dance between the realms of fiction and reality that unfolds within these pages.

This narrative came into existence as a result of my travels, the people I've met, the emotions I've felt, and the stories that came walking into my life.

May "Anvi" not only entertain but also serve as a catalyst for introspection, encouraging you to navigate the twists and turns of your own life with newfound resilience and understanding.

Acknowledgements

I would like to thank all the people who have contributed to the creation of this book, giving me inspiration in the form of their emotions and expressing their vulnerabilities to me.

I'm grateful to the readers who continue to support me with their valuable input and are watching me develop as an author and a poet.

Also, once again, thank you, God, for blessing me with the gift of expression.

CHAPTER ONE

RETURNING HOME

The little girl stood near the dimly lit lamp, ashamed of the situation she found herself in. She felt alone, naked—as if clothes were being removed from her body, one garment at a time.

Her father was sitting in his huge chair, with the right leg crossed on top of the left one. His Thakur pride was getting stronger with age, maybe due to insecurities arising from brittle bones and backaches.

"Anvi, tell me what happened right this instant," asked a slightly angry but mostly offended Raghavendra Singh.

Still in her school dress, Anvi knew her father's anger and was visibly scared and distressed. She was trying to control her shaking body, trying to bring her emotions under control.

How can a middle-aged man, being a government official with a reputed designation, understand the emotions of a girl studying in the third grade when Anvi herself couldn't comprehend what had happened to her?

In front of Raghavendra was the father of a boy, Shivansh, slightly older than Anvi. One would conclude from the situation that the boy and the girl had gotten into a fight like kids do and ended up dirtying their clothes or hurling verbal abuse.

"He, he held me and gave me a kiss on the lips, like they do in the movies," said a scared and stuttering Anvi. "I hated it."

"No one can clap with a single hand, *Singh Sahab*," immediately Shivansh's father defended his only son. "There is something more to the story that these two are not wishing to tell."

Giving a little slap on Shivansh's cheek, his father asked him if he liked Anvi and if the two were in a relationship.

"These kids nowadays are increasingly influenced by cinema, *Singh Sahab*. You need to control your girl or she'll destroy your pride," Shivansh's father aggressively suggested. "Boys can do what they feel like, and no one will bat an eye, but your girl is so little, you need to control her."

Raghavendra, the sole male in the house, was never good with emotions, but when it came to his pride, any threat must be eliminated. He took his family from a city with ice-cold yet heavenly mountains and clear-running rivers to a small, congested town because of his job, leaving behind the family that he prioritized over his wife and children.

"I apologize on behalf of my spoiled child," Raghavendra said. "She's good at studying, so I guess I've been letting her watch too much television."

An expression of relief took over the father-son duo, who were eager to get over the matter as soon as possible. They knew they had their victory in the bag.

After Shivansh and her father left, Raghavendra tightly held his daughter's right arm, dragging her to a room and giving an 8-year-old a slap that felt like a brick being mashed into one's face. Anvi fell, immediately sobbing as her mother watched *Singh Sahab* beat a child who didn't even know what romantic relations are or what kisses represented.

Those were the times when smartphones were almost absent, and even teenagers relied on movies to understand their urges. Raghavendra failed to realize that his child was not grown up but was still trying to process the bad touches that cursed her body from early childhood.

Raghavendra started rigorously searching for something. His heavy steps pushed the ground underneath him as he walked into his room. Moments later, he came out with a scissor. Anvi's elder sister and mother were concerned but lacked the courage to speak.

He held Anvi's hair tightly in his hand, cutting them off, relieving the child of her biggest treasure. She cried continuously the whole day, and soon, the tears stopped pouring down, giving up their hope for mercy.

After *Singh Sahab* left the house, Anvi's mother arranged her hair, trimming down the uneven strands, explaining how she angered her father by getting involved with a guy.

"You're still too young for such things, and your father works very hard to provide for us. You should be grateful to him and protect his pride," said Anvi's mother.

The night ended with Anvi realizing that something had broken inside for her, opening the door for a feeling of emptiness that would possess her for years.

A few days passed, and Anvi was back to school with bruises. Shivansh and his friends continued to indulge in non-consensual touches, while Anvi decided to never speak a word about any of it, to anyone. She gave priority to protecting her father's pride and tried fighting the worst men on her own.

Things that were bad before Shivansh and his father visited Raghavendra's house turned worse. The nightmare only ended once *Singh Sahab* shifted to a major city from the small town they used to live in, with Anvi stomaching secrets that would possibly suffocate a barrel that didn't have a bottom.

Raghavendra's brother also followed him, settling in the city at a nearby location.

Fast forward years Anvi is now a grown woman aspiring to become a big-shot architect and has moved to an even bigger city for her job.

She still hasn't been able to figure out whether her father cared for her or not. Some questions and their answers end up in the grave, taking the beating of time and remaining in silence for eternity.

***

"Where are you, Anvi? You'll miss the train if you don't hurry up! It's Diwali, and if you don't reach on time, you know your father will get angry," Anvi's mother said on a call.

"I'm on the way, but the traffic in these big cities is suffocating," she replied.

Anvi knew she couldn't miss the train, or else there'd be consequences.

She had started working as an intern at an architecture firm, and she had been living away from home for the first time in the past year. While the world might be brutal, professional experiences are fucked up as well—a human can't catch a break!

She has grown her hair back and wears it like a crown. A peculiar habit she developed while coming to the new city was smoking.

People perceive smoking as a fatal habit, but it's much more than that. No one smokes because it's fun; people smoke because it is the closest thing to the euphoric feeling of happiness.

The traffic refused to clear up, and rolling down the windows of her Uber, Anvi could see a person on a huge motorcycle arguing with a car driver who rear-ended him. She was trying to get a good look at the motorcycle, a dream purchase for her.

"Can I smoke?" Anvi asked the driver, who gave his approval while taking out his own cigarette.

Back when she was in 12th grade, Anvi and her cousin, Rishabh, took her father's new motorcycle on a ride when he was off to work.

"It's amazing, isn't it, riding a motorcycle?" Rishabh asked. "The feeling of freedom, anxiety, and a chronic rush attacking you at once is just marvelous!"

"I know!" Anvi shouted while sitting at the back. "Would you teach me?"

"Well, you're taking responsibility if something happens, 'cause it's your father's bike," Rishabh replied.

"I'd like to learn and surprise him," an excited Anvi said.

Two days passed by, with Anvi finally learning the basics of motorcycling. The third day, Rishabh and Anvi decided to showcase her new skills in front of the family.

It was almost afternoon, and Raghavendra used to come home for lunch around 3 in the afternoon. Rishabh was already waiting for Anvi at home, stopping her father from going inside with short conversations.

"You know, I've heard girls are also driving bikes nowadays," said Rishabh while throwing a piece of round rock a few feet away from Raghavendra with a Satanic smile.

A few moments later, Raghavendra's bike could be seen and heard on the horizon. Anvi was driving well but was unable to stomach her excitement, wondering what a proud Thakur father with no son and two daughters would look like.

The bike's speed was quite slow, and as Anvi neared Raghavendra, the motorcycle's handle became unstable due to a round rock on the ground, throwing the girl off the seat.

The motorcycle immediately fell, suffering from a few scratches and indicators falling apart. Rishabh ran towards Anvi, helping her stand up. A furious Raghavendra, who was feeling a little warm for her little girl a short while ago, was now furious with rage.

"The fuck do you think you were doing?" Raghavendra said. He slapped his daughter as hard as he could, throwing her down the memory lane of the third standard. Anvi ran inside as fast as she could, while Raghavendra picked up his motorcycle.

"Did you teach her to ride Rishabh?" asked Raghavendra.

"I didn't want to, but she wouldn't stop complaining and threatened me that she would spread rumors about me," said Rishabh. "I had no options!"

"What should I do with this girl? Why didn't I get a boy like you as my son?" Raghavendra said.

***

An hour passed, and the argument between the biker and the car owner subsided. The train would leave in half an hour, while the Uber driver informed her that it would take at least forty minutes to reach the destination.

Anvi had a feeling that she was screwed. One way or another, she had to reach home before the sun came out the next day.

Forty minutes pass easily when you're listening to your favorite songs or wondering if life is even worth living. But when you're in a hurry, time suddenly slows down, creating its very own subdivisions. One can notice every minute detail in such moments.

Reaching the station, Anvi saw a long queue for luggage check-in, another hurdle. She could hear the announcement that the train was standing on the platform and would leave in a minute. She held her bag close to her bosom and ran as fast as she could, pushing everyone away. Her phone was ringing in her pocket, but she paid no attention to it.

Making her way to the platform, Anvi realized that the train had started to move and tried her best to catch up with it, but to no avail. She ran behind it, giving up eventually.

A hand crept up on Anvi's shoulders, and it was her elder sister.

"You came late! I had to get off. I'll tell my father that it wasn't my fault," Jhanvi said.

"We have to reach home by tomorrow; let's take a bus!" Anvi replied, knowing that she was doomed.

The duo hurriedly worked their way towards the bus stand, which was quite close. Meanwhile, Anvi's phone had been ringing continuously. Twenty minutes passed, the tickets were booked, and Anvi finally took out her phone. There were four missed calls from Rishabh. She called back.

"Brooo! You didn't pick up. I'm in a pickle and need a thousand rupees immediately. Could you send the money over?" Rishabh asked.

"You only miss me when you need money, right?" Anvi said.

"I'll gift you something good this birthday, I promise! It's coming, right? Let me guess, umm, I forgot, but I know it's in February!" Rishabh said. "Please help me out."

Anvi checked her account balance, and it had only 1200 INR in it. She sent Rishabh 1000 INR, buying snacks for her sister and herself with the leftovers.

The two sisters were waiting for the bus to take off when Jhanvi's phone rang.

"It's father," Jhanvi told Anvi.

"Hello father! Yeah, I got to the platform on time, but Anvi came late, so I had to get off. We've taken the bus, and we'll meet you at home," Jhanvi said.

"Your mother and I are going to my brother's today. They have a ceremony, and we'll stay there for a few days. I expect you to reach home and find your way to your uncle's. Tell your sister the same!" Raghavendra said.

"We're fucked, aren't we?" Anvi asked her sister.

"Maybe!" Jhanvi replied.

The bus swayed left and right as cold air poured in from the sides, pushing Anvi towards thoughts of a broken past. It wasn't that she never felt loved. She had her fair share of suitors over the years, but things ended with her saying, "*Mai kaat dungi tumhara!* (I'll break your heart)."

She fell in and out of love with people, discovering her romantic side. Her first few months in the big city included a few trips to clubs, some new romantic encounters, and a realization that money might be a way out of all the problems in life.

Loud music, people dancing all around—she felt disconnected from herself in clubs, subduing the emotional need to be loved. In the new city, Anvi's secret smoking sessions turned into a full-blown habit as she witnessed how people kept up with the fast pace of life.

***

The sun was almost up, and the duo was about to reach their destination. Anvi knew that things wouldn't be okay with her father when she returned, but she was at peace knowing that she now had a life of her own—she could escape.

"*Didi*, we are about to reach," Anvi said while waking her sister up with a strong pinch.

"Oww!" Jhanvi shouted while hitting her sister.

Jhanvi, the firstborn daughter of Raghavendra, had given up on the struggles of her home a long time ago. She knew how to avoid tense situations, while Anvi was more of a rebel, constantly claiming attention in her home.

Raghavendra wants to get her first-born daughter married as soon as possible and is constantly in search of a suitor.

An Indian father is often preoccupied with his daughter's marriage from quite a young age, getting emotional at the thought of his daughter leaving his household. However, the same father is distant when it comes to understanding the needs, wants, and situations of his daughter.

"You might like the same pinch after you get married," Anvi teased her elder sister.

Jhanvi was visibly upset with the comment. There was some secret eating her from within.

"There's a guy back in the city that I like, but I don't think that father would like him. He's from a different caste and is not a hotshot," Jhanvi expressed her concern.

"Maybe I can try talking to him?" Anvi suggested.

"You'd be the last person to motivate Raghavendra Singh," Jhanvi retorted.

"Excuse me," an old man sitting in front of the two sisters said.

"Sorry to meddle, but I have a daughter just like you, and I couldn't help but hear your conversation. I would suggest that you just accept the decisions that your parents make. They always know what's better for you," he said.

"Yeah, I believe you to be right," Jhanvi said.

"The fuck! He is not right. With all due respect, you don't know shit about our situation. Kindly mind your own business. I think my sister is wise enough to choose a man who loves her," an angry Anvi said.

Parents are always right. A saying that has burned innumerable dreams, cost countless lives, and left many speechless is running deep inside the nubile minds of millions of Indians.

The bus stopped, pushing everyone to move forward. Anvi and Jhanvi reached their destination and knew how to make their way back home. To their surprise, one of the cousins was standing, rolling his car keys in his hands, waiting for his sisters, and singing an unforgettable tune:

"A fire has been burning for years, endless,
Two sticks have been chosen for the sacrifice, priceless.
Away from the tree, they had the world to roam,
Dear sisters, I congratulate you on returning home."

CHAPTER TWO

ROTTEN RELATIONS

Stepping foot in the city that you once considered home but now cannot wait to part ways with is a curse. Anvi, back in her hometown, was unexpectedly occupied by the memories that forced open a gaping hole in her heart.

"Welcome, Anvi and Jhanvi. I hope you have a lot of stories for me and my friend," Shivam, the cousin, said.

Shivam came with a friend of his, Anurag. The two had been best pals since childhood and shared everything with each other.

While Anurag was nowhere to be seen, Anvi, tired from a long and arduous journey, asked Shivam to drop them off at the house instantly.

"We need to reach our uncle's before their ceremony begins, and I don't want to hear any sarcastic comments from father," said a tired Anvi.

"Let's wait for Anurag. He was just around the corner," Shivam argued.

A few minutes later, Anurag came out of hiding with a rose and a sunflower, handing each to Anvi and Jhanvi, respectively.

"A rose for Anvi; what's cooking here?" Shivam questioned.

"Nothing, just a nice gesture," a hesitant Anurag replied.

Well, it wasn't 'nothing.' There was something much larger at play here that Anvi knew the moment she saw the rose.

A few years ago, Anvi came to know that Anurag was head over heels for her and tried to bribe her cousin to set up meetings.

"*Mai tumhara kaat hi dungi* (I'll break your heart); so let's go before I lose my mind," a visibly irritated Anvi told Anurag.

Anurag felt a little sad, but he was accustomed to such rejections from Anvi over the years. Shivam brought over the car, and the other three sat in the vehicle, driving off towards Anvi's home.

"I'm opening the windows," Anvi exclaimed.

She liked watching buildings pass by swiftly, one-by-one, each with their own stories, their own struggles, and a lifestyle completely different from hers.

"If only I could bum a cigarette and not get caught," Anvi wondered.

"A city can change beyond recognition in a year, but the people in it remain the same," Anvi thought to herself as a shop passed by where she used to hang out with her school best friend.

Time flies faster than thought. Or maybe the rules of time are not applicable when a person is nostalgic?

As Anvi got closer and closer to her house, a school passed by. A plethora of faces crossed her mind in a flash—the teachers, the friends, the enemies, and the lovers—all lost in the sea of passing time.

"Oh, how I used to wait to see the face of an idiotic crush for so long while he was busy making out with my best friend. I wonder what they both are up to nowadays," Anvi thought.

People often take for granted how situations and people transform in a short span of time. Out of sight, out of mind—a century-old saying that stands true now more than ever.

Ten more minutes, and the car would reach its destination.

"Don't you live here, Anurag?" Anvi suddenly said.

"Yeah, yeah. I'll get off. Stop the car, Shivam," Anurag said.

"Don't forget your end of the deal," Shivam reminded Anurag.

The more you chase love, the further it goes away from you. Anurag tried to chase and capture a wind that was never his to begin with. Every damn time, he ended up breaking his heart after pumping it with false expectations.

The car stopped.

"Here we are," Shivam said. "I fulfilled your father's wishes, and he has asked me to tell you that the ceremony is in the evening, and you both are expected to arrive at the scene in an hour or two at most."

Anvi opened the vehicle's door with a deep sigh, and Jhanvi was already inside, getting ready to avoid angering her father.

The car left with Anvi standing in front of her house with two large bags and a heavy heart.

"So, we meet again. Here I thought that I had escaped my nightmare," Anvi said.

What Anvi did not know was that the next few days would change her life forever. The rotten relationships that were developed under the pressure of obedience would finally break.

***

Anvi entered her house via the main door, dragging two of her bags, wondering where time went. The walls changed their appearance and color, yet the faint redolence of Raghavendra's tobacco pipes stayed deep into their pores.

The ancient Thakur relics depicting the bravery of a long-lost civilization would strike fear in the hearts of guests. No matter how much Anvi tried to pretend to be a guest, she was an integral part of the structure's foundation.

A shield with swords crossing over from each side reminded Anvi of his father's old and strong pride.

She could feel a sudden gust of wind, warning her of an incoming change, a possible dilemma, or a forthcoming incident. She never wanted to come back, but she had to anyway.

Jhanvi, on the other hand, was prepped and ready to go. Meanwhile, Anvi's mind was preoccupied with thoughts of the past, with scars that never healed, and with sorrows that were never transformed into tears.

"Anvi. Anvi!" Jhanvi repeatedly called her sister. "Let's go! We're going to be late, and you know, Papa."

"Yeah, give me a minute," Anvi said.

She went into her room. While the room was cleaned regularly, no one touched the items kept in there.

A bed, where she lay sleepless most nights, knitting elaborate dreams and plans for the future. A mirror where she held her beautiful locks of hair that were brutally removed from her head. A bathroom where she burned all the letters she received from her suitors and lovers. Finally, a table where she gave it all to fulfill her father's wishes but was never able to live the life that her peers enjoyed.

People inside wealthy houses can be unhappy too. Money was never the measure of wealth; it was always a tool of exchange.

Anvi opened her bedside drawer, fishing for something important. The drawer was empty, as was the one on the other side of the bed. She hurriedly opened her table drawer, feeling satisfied after finding a bunch of papers folded together.

"Anvi, I need you to dress faster," Jhanvi shouted.

"Yeah, yeah," Anvi murmured.

She took out the papers, unfolding them. These papers were her treasure, containing emotions that poured out in the form of art.

Art only comes when the mind and the heart are in strife and the struggle suffocates a person's soul. A few years ago, Anvi picked up the habit of drawing what came into her mind. Her mother would occasionally praise her, but when the hobby became a regular affair, Raghavendra stepped in.

In eighth standard, Anvi's grades started deteriorating amid internal struggles. The lower her grades went, the more Raghavendra would scold and sometimes hit her, restricting her time with friends, especially boys.

"Stop fucking over your life. A few years down the road, and you'd wish you had listened to your father," Raghavendra said after the ninth standard annual student report.

Anvi found peace in knowing that she could always pour her feelings into a piece of paper and forget about the constant battle that her head and heart were in.

She went through her drawings, and a single drop of tears tumbled down her cheeks. Memories are a treacherous trap; sometimes they can feel euphoric, and sometimes they can hurt like a third-degree burn.

"Anvi! Come out now!" Jhanvi shouted at the top of her lungs.

***

Anvi came out a few minutes later, a black *kurti* adorning her body. She applied a splash of red lipstick to her lips and wore a small black *bindi* on her forehead. A silver bangle on her left hand only upscaled her appearance as she prepared her pride—her hair.

There are celebrations for joyous occasions that you are invited to but would rather miss out on. Anvi liked dressing up, but when it came to a family function surrounded by many unknown creatures, her heart sank, creating a picture-perfect fake smile that would confuse even the wisest of suitors.

Her elegance was unparalleled among all her relatives. Anvi was blessed with a subtle yet tragic beauty that would settle in the eyes of the person looking at her. Her eyes, adorned with *kajal*, were laden with innocence and excuses, like those of a deer hiding in the jungle, afraid to confront humans or animals.

Her neck, carved beautifully by the Creator with the most fragile and yet elegant of elements, boasted a thin silver necklace, which was hidden underneath her bosom to some extent.

Anvi's ears carried black earrings that completed the palazzos she was wearing beneath her *kurti*, hiding the bewitching legs that seemed like they were sculpted with the clay found on the bank of the Ganges.

In a final touch, Anvi carefully pushed her hair around her neck, landing the lochs on her bosom while stretching her arms where any man would give up his earthly possessions to lay his head in a state of eternal peace.

"Let's go now. I've called an Uber," Jhanvi said.

They got into the cab, and the drop-off was just a few minutes away. It had been a year since Anvi and Raghavendra saw each other. Some part of the little girl wanted the father to acknowledge her presence, to hug her with warmth, and to address her with the love that she never got.

Raghavendra was a different person in front of the world. He was respected by every cousin and family member for his honesty, his girls, who were growing to be beautiful, and his paternal wealth. *Singh Sahab* has the reputation of a king, and he has earned the respect of everyone, but today he was going to fall in the eyes of his daughter.

The sisters stepped out of the cab, entering a well-lit house crowded with people and embellished with flowers, incense, and pictures of Hindu gods.

"My two little princesses have arrived!" exclaimed Mahendra's wife.

Mahendra was Raghavendra's younger brother, who looked up to his brother and considered the sisters his own daughters. There were cousins all over the place except Rishabh, who was Mahendra's youngest son.

"I wish my son was as obedient as the two of you. That idiot has yet to arrive and asked me for 10,000 INR this morning, saying that he didn't have money for coming home," Mahendra's wife said.

Anvi wondered what Rishabh was doing with all the money he was being sent; he asked for 1000 INR from her as well.

"I thought Rishabh earned quite well," a puzzled Anvi questioned her aunt.

"I really don't understand him. Well, his father and even your father are pretty proud of him. Maybe he's doing something right that the two brothers' would only know," the aunt said while running away to prepare for the ceremony.

There was hubbub all around, with each person talking to another while sipping tea and coffee. Everyone had something to say about the other—some good, some bad.

Perspective is an ornament, a luxury only worn by those who are shattered.

After catching up with relatives, Jhanvi and Anvi got separated while looking for their parents. Gradually, the sun decided to go into deep slumber as night took over. A hungry Anvi took a few *laddoos* for herself and decided to savor the delicacy of alienation.

Out of the blue came a small monkey, brown in color, gifted a red butt by the Creator, searching for food. After being chased away by everyone in the party, the closest relative to humans sat at the feet of the Anvi, gazing at the little bites that the lady took.

"You hungry, little fella?" Anvi questioned while giving away a *laddoo*.

The monkey immediately took the offer, running away with the item. Anvi decided to chase the animal, considering that she had nothing better to do. The chase ended a few seconds later when the monkey sat on top of a car.

Inside the car, Anvi saw her cousins and a bottle of liquor in the hands of one of them. She rushed over.

"So, what is going on here?" Anvi asked.

"Well, the ceremony got boring. If you keep quiet, we'll give you some as well," said Anurag, who was also seated in the back with Shivam.

"Umm, by any chance, do you guys have a cigarette as well?" Anvi asked.

"Sure, sure," an ecstatic Shivam said.

Anvi got into the car, immediately took the bottle, and drank a significant amount of liquor straight from the bottle. She proceeded to snatch a cigarette from Shivam and take a deep draw from the butt of the cancer stick, exhaling the smoke a few seconds later.

She got what she wanted: a few minutes of relief and the courage to face her father. Anvi filled her mouth with snacks that were kept in the car to layer her mouth's odor with other fragrances while opening the car's door and leaving.

"What the fuck was that?" a puzzled Shivam wondered.

Meanwhile, Anurag watched Anvi leave with a sigh as everyone in the car started teasing him over his unrequited love. Everyone wondered when the lady started drinking and smoking, but they kept their mouths shut and continued their little party.

"She breaks my heart again and again, and I just love it," Anurag wondered.

On the other hand, Anvi was a little drunk, but not enough. She could still feel, think, and be in her senses.

"Maybe I should've had more," Anvi thought.

A few minutes later, she went inside a room and found her father, mother, Mahendra, and his wife talking. The four were engaged in a hearty conversation that simmered down when Anvi entered the room.

"Anvi, how have you been, my child?" her mother asked.

"*Bhabhiji*, we met earlier and had a good chat. She's such a good daughter!" Mahendra's wife said.

Raghavendra remained silent.

"Namaste, Papa," said Anvi in an awkward voice.

Raghavendra turned to Mahendra and asked when the main event of the ceremony would begin.

"In an hour, I believe. We are waiting for the bastard Pandit," said Mahendra.

"So, Anvi, how was the journey? I thought you'd be here in the morning, but it turns out you were way late," questioned Mahendra.

"Well, you know, there was a popular saying that your late grandmother used to say. Would you like to hear?" Mahendra asked.

"Yes, please," said Anvi.

Mahendra quoted:

"There are three kinds of idiots living on this plane:
One with lots of wealth but working for gain,
One with lots of luck but bad decisions, going insane;
One who is so absent that she misses her train."

CHAPTER THREE

FALLING FROM GRACE

A dreadful silence occupied Anvi's mind while an idiotic grin appeared on Mahendra's face. Raghavendra, upset with his daughter for missing the train, remained muted.

Anger replaces love when it assumes total control. The affection that Raghavendra might've felt while seeing his daughter after almost a year was overshadowed by the rage that forms when a stubborn man is fixated on a minute event that did not go according to his expectations.

People say that expectation kills peace of mind. Anvi expected her father to side with him after Mahendra's sarcastic comment, but, to her surprise, Raghavendra's lips were sealed shut by his anger.

"She couldn't get one thing right, getting me ridiculed at a place where I'm well-respected," Raghavendra thought to himself.

On the contrary, Anvi wondered if her father was capable of preserving the pride of his daughter in front of people who barely mattered in her life.

"Well, at least I'm here, aren't I?" Anvi spoke a few minutes later. "Where's Rishabh, your well-mannered son, by the way?"

Raghavendra, shocked at the sudden tiff and sarcastic reply from his daughter, gave an eye to his wife.

"Anvi, let's go and eat something. You must be hungry, and we have a lot of food," her mother said while taking Anvi out of that room.

Anvi and her mother left, while Raghavendra and Mahendra continued their conversation.

"I think that your younger daughter is getting out of hand. I advised you against sending her to the city, but you were adamant on making her a big-shot architect. Well, at the rate she's growing, she might bring her own man one day, asking for your blessings," Mahendra said.

Raghavendra had no response to this unnecessary advice shared by Mahendra, whose ego was obviously hurt by Anvi's blunt remarks.

On the other hand, Anvi's already injured heart was stabbed once again by the lack of support shown by her father. She expected her father to support the reply she gave after the brutal and sarcastic remarks shared by Mahendra.

The most fucked-up thing is that this world is expecting things to change after a prolonged period of no contact when the foundations were faulty.

Anvi, Jhanvi, and their mother were sitting in silence, having tea and *samosas*.

Not long after, the ceremony began, and Jhanvi and her mother left while supposedly talking about how Anvi created a mess in front of her uncle and father.

"This isn't the first time he has let me down. Every damn time I expect him to be a little more human, he turns out to be more of an asshole. What is wrong with his head?" Anvi thought to herself while thinking about all the times she felt let down by Raghavendra.

It is said that father-daughter relationships are the most special because a father is the first male that a girl encounters in her life.

But isn't it ironic that a father can be the most inexpressive being while a daughter can be the most emotionally demanding one?

People often wish that their parents used their emotions and not their minds while parenting. However, by the time the mom and dad get old, they fall from the grace of their children.

Anvi's mind was a raging shitstorm. More importantly, she had given up on her mother getting involved in any of the matters concerning her husband's pride.

Aarti, born 55 years ago in a hospital to a government official and a housewife, was married to Raghavendra at an early age. She was the eldest in her home, and paved the way for her younger sisters to get educated and work reputed jobs by getting married first.

Women are perceptive, and after being married for decades, Aarti stopped meddling in the affairs of her husband. Who knows what made her give up?

Every relationship is a house of cards, with each card laden with a specific memory. The web that joins these cards is fragile, and once broken, the relationship only survives on said memories while the affection dies.

So, here Anvi was sitting alone, with a sister that was loyal to her father, a mother that rarely spoke against Raghavendra, and a father that had a pride as fragile as a drunk man's ego.

***

The ceremony was finally over, and people were going home with fat bellies and entertained minds. What has changed over thousands of years of evolution? People still gather at huge parties, share food, talk, and forget the mess that their lives are in.

Soon, the only people left at the party were relatives. It was time for Raghavendra and his family to leave as well.

"Accha, congratulations on the successful ceremony. Let us all meet on Diwali and play cards," Raghavendra said while retracing his steps towards the outer gate.

Everyone exchanged goodbyes, and Raghavendra brought the car out. Everyone got in, with Aarti seated in the front passenger seat and Jhanvi and Anvi seated in the back.

Anvi's bold remarks a few hours earlier spread like wildfire throughout the family. People were talking, and Raghavendra knew.

The serene environment in the car was an invitation for one of the four people to break the silence. Raghavendra, the head of the family, decided to pierce the stillness in the air.

"After spending a year in the big city, it seems that someone has lost all respect for elders. I never thought one of my daughters would blabber whatever comes to her mind to people who have seen life much more than her," a pissed-off father said. "Your mother talks more with the two of you, so I don't meddle much. But it seems that she is not doing that good of a job at parenting nowadays. There are ways in which you behave in society. You do not come from a lineage of *rickshawalas*."

Anvi opened the car's window, gazing at the moon, wondering if she should have cited a reason to not come home and just stay in the city.

Your life might seem normal when you're at home, but once you meet others at your job or college and share your personal thoughts and experiences, your horizons widen. Anvi realized in the past 365 days that what she lived through was an average experience for a girl but concluded that it was wrong.

Cars passed, markets faded, and Anvi continued to look outside the window while her father continued to rain like dogs and cats on her.

"If only I could go to a club and dance my heart out!" She wished. "Well, it doesn't matter. Just two more days of this torture."

"Instead of spending all that money on you, we should've bought a dog; after all, you've been looking outside the vehicle just like a canine in a car," Raghavendra said.

Passing judgments is the sole goal of life for those who believe themselves to be above the people that surround them.

It is very easy to judge the people in the plains while sitting on the edge of a mountain, but once you are deprived of the clear air and subjected to constant corporate exploitation, what is the difference?

Call it an influence of alcohol or a maturing mindset, Anvi did not want to overlook the last remark. Her retortion was unexpected and would silence Raghavendra's tongue for days to come.

***

"You know what? No matter how much you convince yourself, you're not the 'Father of the Year' hell; you're not even 'Father of the Day.' What have you done all your life except NOT TAKE MY SIDE? You saw your little daughter after a year, and all you had to convey was anger! I'm habitual of taking shit from you, but not from your brother!" Anvi said.

Anvi's throat started to feel heavy. She had been holding back for far too long, and little drops of tears poured down her left cheek. Her heart started to beat faster, the mind telling her to keep the mouth shut while the statements generated from replayed scenarios in the mind continued to pour out.

"You were not man enough to take your daughter's side when your own brother belittled her, and you talk about your Thakur pride? What is the point of raising daughters and expecting a husband to protect her when you've not been able to do the same?" Anvi added.

Jhanvi immediately rubbed her elbows against Anvi, asking her to silence her anger. However, Anvi was far from done. The thoughts that had been eating her since long begged to come out, while her logical brain entreated Anvi to keep shut, knowing there was no benefit from this argument.

Raghavendra went silent and focused on driving his car. But his ears were wide open, his heart heavy, and he knew he had let his daughter down.

Realization is not a punctual entity; it comes late when things are too broken to amend.

"Don't you have anything to say, Papa?" Anvi questioned. "I know you won't say shit. You know why? Because silence is the only answer you have. It'd be easier if you had a son instead of me, or maybe he might also turn into a narcissist like you."

"Anvi enough!" Aarti said.

"Your father has done enough for the three of us. He gave us a house, put both of you through school and college, and tried his best to protect you from the outside world. You should be thankful to us; we sacrificed our lives to give you the best as per our resources. If our parents were alive, you'd know what true fear meant," Anvi's mother continued.

Raghavendra slowly made a turn and stopped his car on the side of the road. Turning the ignition off, he looked at his wife.

"There is no end to this debate. After all, when children grow up, their first task is to rebel against their parents and try to make them understand how they failed to raise their children," Raghavendra said in a grave voice.

"When I was young, I had a similar conversation with my father that ended up with him bruising my face for the next week. Before we resume our journey, I'd like to tell you both that I did the best I could as per my understanding, and down the road, you will know that your parents were always right," he added.

"Oh right? You cut my hair, made hell of my entire college life, and restricted my breathing. You know what? The day I left for the city, I never felt so free from your corrupt grip," a sobbing Anvi added. "In the end, your explanations are nothing but a false attempt to save your pride, an effort to continue believing that you were a good father."

"You had the entire world in mind—your relatives, friends, et cetera—while raising me, but I only had you. You raised me in a way that would lead to your peers respecting you, but my individuality perished in the fire of your shallow ego," Anvi said while taking a deep breath.

Everyone in the car was quiet as a stillness seeped into the cold air that turned warm with rage, regret, and emotions. The truth is harsh, and even harsher are the facts. What Anvi presented were facts, but when spoken with anger, truth and facts lose their substance.

The car's engine came to life with what seemed like a roar amid an eerie silence. The journey continued, with each person quelling the emotions in their heavy hearts. The journey, which was just ten minutes long, felt like an hour.

As Diwali approached, Anvi was taciturn and morose with the other family members. The celebrations turned into a problem as loads of guests stopped by, dropping gifts like pigeons dropping their shit on people's heads.

The firecrackers didn't feel amusing, the *meethais* didn't feel sweet enough, and the games were not entertaining for anyone living inside the home built by Raghavendra years ago. On the other hand, winter was approaching, bearing a cold and horrific message.

The brightness of the house ironically reflected the darkness inside. But the question was, would things change?

Soon, Diwali was over, and it was time for Anvi to return to the big city. Jhanvi had already left with a heavy heart, and both the mother and the father, along with Anvi, bid her goodbye. Meanwhile, the very next day, Anvi had reserved a train early in the morning.

Aarti came out to bid her daughter goodbye, while Raghavendra was nowhere to be seen. The mother-daughter duo waited for him but finally gave up.

"I guess Papa is still pissed off, and why wouldn't he be? It takes a strong man to accept his mistakes, and maybe he isn't the superhero that I always felt the need to impress," Anvi told her mother.

"You shouldn't talk about your father like that. One fine day, when you'll become a parent, you'll realize how flawed your perspective was," Aarti said.

"I know I'd be a shitty parent, so I don't want to be one. I don't want to get married either. It'd be better if you convey that to your husband as well," Anvi said while getting into a cab that had arrived a few minutes ago.

"Bye, Mummy," Anvi said with a warm stomach as the car started to move forward.

As she looked back, Anvi could see that her father was on the balcony with his hands behind his back, looking at the vehicle as it drove away. Anvi immediately turned around and broke down.

"Madame, is everything okay?" The puzzled driver asked.

"Yeah, I'm just returning to the city, so I'm feeling a little sad," Anvi replied.

"I once drove your father around the town, and I was pretty sad because my daughter went to college. *Singh Sahab* told me that kids who grow up with love and comfort often find the world confusing and return home. But it is imperative for them to leave the nest so that they can do better than we did," the driver said while turning on the radio, humming a song as the two left.

"The bird created a nest, each day a little bit,
It wasn't the best, but the bird never quit.
The time came for the fledglings to go,
The bird stayed behind, watching its hatchlings grow."

CHAPTER FOUR

THE SUNGLASSES

Once people transition from a controlled environment to freedom, they tend to leave their common sense in the way.

Anvi entered her flat, immediately opened the pack of cigarettes that she had purchased after reaching the city, and burned one of them. To her surprise, she lit the end that was supposed to go in between the lips.

"Ah shit! Where's your brain's at, Anvi?" She thought.

It was clear that her mind was engaged in a troublesome thought, but she tried to avoid it instead of addressing it. She took out another cigarette and burned it, calling one of her few friends, Apurva.

"Have you arrived yet?" Anvi asked.

"Yeah, I'm on my way. So what's the plan for today?" Apurva asked.

"I was going to ask you the same question," Anvi replied.

"Um, let me come over, and we'll decide. Today's Friday, so maybe we can hit a club? Meet some cuties; what else?" Apurva suggested.

"Sounds good; now run your ass here," Anvi said while cutting the call.

She sat on her bed, and without taking off her shoes, Anvi laid down, opening social media on her smartphone, scrolling aimlessly, and watching the lives of her peers. Some were happy in a relationship, some were enjoying a party in a foreign country, while others were slam-dunking their vodka shots.

There were multiple messages from Anvi's suitors, but she refrained from replying to them.

"What's the point? They're all losers anyway," Anvi thought to herself while waiting for her friend to arrive so that the duo could go and party in a club.

Under the influence of alcohol, every person seems good. Emotions are heightened, and people seem trustworthy. The availability of resources at disposal results in casual encounters that might be regretted later.

A minute later, Anvi's phone rang. It was from her father, and she panicked. The call was missed the first time, but the second time the phone rang, she picked it up instantly.

"Hello," Anvi said.

"Are you doing well?" Aarti said it from the other side. "I'm calling from your father's phone because mine is not charged."

"Yeah, I'm fine. I'm a little tired, so I'll just eat and sleep the entire evening. Maybe watch a movie if I feel like it," Anvi replied.

"Okay. If you get the time, dial up your sister and maybe have a chat with her as well," Aarti said.

"I'll talk to her tomorrow. I'm too tired for conversations today," Anvi added.

Honestly, Anvi wasn't tired of the journey. But her mind was tired of replaying the same scenario over and over in her head. There are times when the mind just displays the moments lived by an individual, and it can become problematic with time.

Anvi took out another cigarette and started smoking while waiting for her friend and scrolling through social media. If there was a tool that would numb the minds of its users and allow time to pass faster, smartphones would be it.

Fifteen minutes passed by, and Anvi heard a knock on her room's door. Taken aback by the sudden noise, she knew her friend had arrived. She immediately got up from the bed and opened the door, allowing Apurva to enter.

Apurva has been a close friend of Anvi since she arrived in the city. The two had shared some emotional and fun moments and were each other's sole shoulder to cry on for the past few months.

"Bitch, I missed you!" Apurva exclaimed while hugging Anvi. "Tell me all the drama and the ruckus that you created in your family's life that you told me about via text!"

"Naah, I don't want to spoil my mood. I'm just happy to see you, and damn, you're looking like a treat. So, maybe we can just head out and drink our hearts out?" Anvi said.

"Okay, but first, you need to get ready, lady. I'm not taking you out looking like this. You need to loosen up a little," Apurva replied.

The two went through the entire cabinet that contained Anvi's short collection of casual wear. A dress was decided, and a cab was booked at the same time.

A red dress that ended right around the knees elevated Anvi's beauty. Combined with golden earrings, she looked heavenly.

There was something to her beauty that seeped further away from the traditional mindset of elegance and radiance. The lengthy hair curled behind the ears would even make women jealous. A golden brown hair clamp further brightened the grace of those lustrous locks.

The two friends were now ready for departure, and the driver had already arrived. Anvi was in for a blazing night, forced to confront what she was running from.

***

Anvi and Apurva reached their destination, and the minute they got out of the car, they realized that they had entered a whole new world—a place with bright lights, immense passion, and lustful appearances.

In most places, clubs are 'clubbed' together, making that place a hotspot for potential business deals. The whole area would sparkle like fireflies at night in a secluded village. Loud music occupied the mind, pushing out all ugly thoughts.

"This is what I was talking about!" Anvi exclaimed. "Okay, so let's get into the one with the most crowd and order a few things because I'm getting hungry as hell. Also, let's keep everything under budget."

"'Losing it?' Seems about right," Apurva said while pointing out the club's name.

The loud music was vibrating the ground Anvi and Apurva were walking on. The duo gave their names and contact information to the front desk, stepping foot in a dark world with lights capable of penetrating the eyes.

Office parties were taking place in one corner, while in another corner, a group of boys and girls, possibly meeting for the first time, were blindly tasting what romance felt like for a night under the blanket of intoxication and dim lights.

The drinks were being served uninterrupted, and the smoking room was crowded with casual conversations and blacked-out brains. It takes a few minutes for a person to settle into such an aggressive environment.

Anvi, in her red dress and confident walk, would melt the hearts of those fortunate enough to see her.

Her magical eyes would instill infatuation even in those claiming to have pure souls. Every sound she whispered from her lips flew like roses into the ears of the men surrounding her.

A beauty segregated from the other appealing women in the club, seeing Anvi's hair curled around the waist would make the hearts of many quake with lust.

There was something different about her that night, something that would make many men want to come close to her, talk to her, and dream about her.

"I warn you, don't go hand-in-hand with the first guy you see. There are loads of assholes drunk on testosterone who seek easy sex. So, first hold a conversation and then tread carefully," Apurva advised Anvi.

"Bro, you think I'm an idiot? I've handled worse," Anvi replied. "I'd rip off a guy's face if they thought about some shit."

The two immediately ordered four Long Island iced teas and a non-vegetarian platter. The drinks are always delivered ASAP in clubs, maybe because they'd like you to pay the 400% markup on the liquor prices and regret it a day later.

Fifteen minutes in, and the liquor had already started showing its symptoms as it merged itself with blood to become one. Toxicity in small quantities can be addictive, but once it becomes a way of life, the person is destined to be doomed.

"I feel the liquor kicking in," Apurva said while looking at Anvi, who was nodding her head in appreciation.

The song, the smoke, the ambience, the attention, and the tenebrous atmosphere made Anvi's heart bounce and enveloped her mind in an euphoric feeling, somewhat like serotonin. Suddenly, Anvi felt her heart beat run in symphony with the drums. Everything somehow made sense in the chaos.

More drinks were ordered and consumed, and the two could feel their heads shaking in acceptance of inebriation. Apurva grabbed Anvi's hand as the two left the unfinished food on the table, taking her towards the dance floor.

The two started dancing, pushing their emotions out of their bodies.

"This is one of the best nights ever," Anvi screamed while Apurva smiled and continued dancing in the dark.

A slightly tall, appropriately dressed guy that was sitting in front of the dancing floor smiled at Apurva, suggesting that she was looking nice.

"Call it a hunch or experience; I feel that guy is quite nice, and now I'm going to talk to him. I'd suggest you come with me because I can see he also has a friend," Apurva said.

"Umm, is it really necessary?" Anvi questioned.

"Duh?" Apurva replied while marching towards the stranger.

The stranger and his friend were sitting with drinks and food untouched.

"Are you here to watch women dance?" Apurva boldly questioned. "You two don't seem to be eating or drinking shit."

"Well, we were just going to. Maybe you can help us finish." the stranger said.

"For sure!" Apurva said. "By the way, I'm Apurva, and this is Anvi, my best friend."

"I'm Ravi, and this is Rajat," the stranger replied.

"Nice to meet you, Ravi! So, is there a specific reason why your friend is wearing sunglasses to a club at night?" Anvi asked.

"Excuse me a moment," Rajat said while leaving for the washroom.

"Would you two help me out here? So, Rajat works for a leading consulting firm, and what you need to do is search for a top-tier executive of the firm and pretend to be friends with his wife. Maybe not friends but close relatives, or anything on that line works." Ravi said.

"Why not?" Anvi and Apurva exclaimed.

The three waited eagerly for Rajat to return as they did their research. Meanwhile, more food and drinks were ordered. Rajat returned a few minutes later.

"So, Rajat," Anvi said. "You never told me why you're still stuck to the sunglasses."

"Well, they add mystery to my character, don't they?"

"Maybe," Anvi replied.

"So, Rajat, Ravi told me you work for a big consulting firm. Did you know that the firm's regional manager's wife is a friend of Anvi's mother?" Apurva said.

"You're fucking with me, right?" Rajat said.

"Her name's Rashmi, right? She's my mom's childhood friend. They visit each other frequently," Anvi said.

"Oh fuck!" Rajat said, getting out of the chair. "Anvi ma'am, if you need anything, I'll be your servant today. I'll just forget that I developed an instant crush on you."

"You're quick, boy," Anvi replied with a smile.

The conversations continued as the night went on, with Apurva and Ravi separating from Rajat and Anvi for a little bit of 'alone time.'

Leaving Rajat and Anvi would turn out to be a poor decision on Apurva's part.

Two broken people cannot mend each other's hearts but can only understand the situation the other is in.

***

"So, Anvi, your eyes seem sad; is there anything troubling you?" Rajat asked.

"That's probably how you get girls to talk to you, na?" Anvi joked. "Everybody has a sad story. We all do, and what's sadder is that we all believe our story to be at the bottom on the scale of shittiness."

"Well, if you're still interested, I can tell you the reason behind these sunglasses. Maybe then you can share yours." Rajat said.

"We'll judge that later. So, what's with the sunglasses?" Anvi questioned.

Rajat brought his thumb and index finger together, hesitant to remove his eyewear. A few seconds later, he finally did remove the sunglasses, revealing a nasty scar on his right eye. It seemed like someone shoved their boot into Rajat's face.

"The fuck? Whom did you fight with today?" A puzzled Anvi asked.

"Umm, it's a long story," Rajat replied.

"I'd like to hear a shorter version. It's not like I have something amazing to do right now," Anvi said.

"So, this is a gift from my father," Rajat said.

It was at this moment that Anvi understood she picked the wrong string on the guitar. She was not in the mindset to hear a sad story about how fucked up parents are, but it was a trap she set for herself.

"My father is somewhat of a big shot in my village, and I'm the only son of my parents. He has quite a reach in the entire region and is very well known for drinking his ass off for the past twenty years. For as long as I can remember, my mother and I have been beaten, bruised, and fucked over by my alcoholic, spoilt father," Rajat said.

"Cutting the story short, I went to my village in Diwali to mainly visit my mother and take her to the city with me. Well, my father was not pleased with the idea, and we had a small physical altercation when he was drunk. I went out for a walk to calm myself, and when I returned, I saw my mother being beaten by her husband, who repeatedly said that if she left for the city, he'd find her and kill her," Rajat continued.

Anvi wanted the story to end, for she was in no position to console a man. But she had to hear the end, as she was the one who forced the story out of Rajat. All she could hope for was a positive end so that things could go back to flirting and fun.

"Now, I took my mother from the house and went to the police to complain. The village *policewalas* are useless. They called my father, asking him to keep his son in control because, according to them, I've been 'exposed to the city's air.' He entered, took out his belt, started beating me in front of everyone, and put his boot right here," Rajat said while pointing to his scar.

"My mother promised my father that she wouldn't come with me to the city, and the very next day, I left. Um, here I am, talking to you, bearing the scars of an inhuman father, a cowardly mother, and an intoxicated mind," Rajat said while ending his story.

"I thought that you were slapped by a girl or some shit. This, on the other hand, went way out of hand," Anvi said.

"I think I deserve to know your story too," Rajat said.

Anvi went quiet.

There are two types of stories people like to hear: relatable and understandable. However, when things are too close to real life, such storybooks are closed, hidden behind the curtains of pretense, doubt, and a normal life.

Anvi knew her father was fucked up, and she now found a person in a similar situation. The first thought she had in mind was to run, bid adieu to Rajat, and never see his face again. Why? Maybe because she understood how the man sitting in front of him felt and she saw her own scars that never faded.

"Nope, I'm alright. I think I should be leaving now," Anvi hurriedly said.

"What happened?" A surprised Rajat questioned.

"It's getting late. It was nice seeing you and all, but I really need to go," Anvi said.

"But what about your friend?" Rajat asked.

"She'll find her ride home," Anvi replied, leaving Rajat with some cash for her share of the orders.

"Fuck!" Rajat exclaimed.

Minutes later, Apurva and Ravi came back, laughing and holding each other's hands.

"Where's Anvi?" Apurva asked.

"She left," Rajat said.

"Why?" Apurva questioned.

"I don't know. I just told her the story behind the sunglasses, and she left!" Rajat replied.

Apurva ran outside while assuring Ravi that she would contact him. Meanwhile, Ravi brought Rajat to the side.

"Are you nuts? Who unloads all that garbage the first time you see a girl? Bro, I know you need people to share your emotions, but that doesn't happen in the real world. You need to suck up the shit, build a foundation, and then lay the stones of regret and emotion. If you unload everything at once, people will run away because they have their shit to deal with too! This was so selfish of you, man!"

Ravi said.

People often believe that life works the same as in the movies, but that is not true. People react differently to distinct situations, for everyone is fucked up in the 21st century. Rajat and Ravi quietly started sipping their drinks while wondering the reason behind Anvi's sudden departure.

Rajat was disheartened.

He kept picturing Anvi's eyes flecked with pearlish hues, wondering if he was the one who chased her away, reminiscing about how her pretty smile turned into a poor man's grimace after hearing his story, cursing his heart for revealing the mystery.

CHAPTER FIVE

BREATHING IN A CUBE

Anvi was outside the club, her hands crossed over. She was disturbed, agitated, angry, and sad—all at the same time.

She constantly checked her phone, waiting for her cab driver to come and retrieve her from the hellish thoughts of her past. A few minutes later, Apurva, worried for her friend, came out, calling her name.

"Anvi! What are you doing here? What happened? Did that guy say something? I'll fuck him up!" she said.

"No! He just shared too much, and I can't handle that. Why do men expect women to take care of their selfish asses and relieve them of their trauma? I mean, I have my shit too, and I came to this idiotic place to forget about my fucked-up life and not to listen to another person's fucking story," Anvi replied.

"Maybe men are raised this way? Um, I believe that there is a side to everyone, man or woman, that craves empathy from the person that they start to care about. People need someone to talk to, and that, my friend, is a rarity nowadays. People don't talk anymore; they fuck and leave, or they stay and make your life hell," Apurva said.

The conversation was interrupted by the driver's call, who confirmed his arrival at the location.

"Well, if you are leaving, we can go together. I've taken Ravi's number so we can catch up later, or maybe I'll just ghost him," Apurva said with a not-so-funny face.

The cab stopped in front of them, and the two girls got in, tired and exasperated, wondering how an awesome night ended with a question mark.

Anvi took her head out of the car's window, reminiscing about a small quote that she created to settle her emotions when they went out of control a few years ago:

"Paradise was a place that I was living in, and yet, I consider it a hell;

Paradise was a place I was crying for, and in a paradise of my own, I fell."

"That's true," Apurva said. "But, babe, you need to chill out. You're spiraling down the rabbit hole that will fuck you up in your intoxicated state. We often make regretful mistakes under alcohol, lol."

"What happens when you ask your family for an opinion?" Anvi asked.

"What?" Apurva retorted with another question.

"You get eight," Anvi said.

Apurva sighed and closed her eyes, asking the cab driver to turn up the 80s song that he was playing.

Intoxication is like holding a stick that has a nail protruding out—the emotion you carry in your heart will continue to intensify until the drowsiness sets in.

Anvi's hair went haywire as she closed her eyes and rested her head on the car's door. She could feel the cold breeze hugging her face and neck, taking her back a few years, when she used to cry for the very air of freedom that she was trying to enjoy to the fullest.

***

The tenth standard board exams were on Anvi's head, and the curse of love entered her life for the first time. It wasn't that she never felt anything for a boy before, but for the first time, she loved herself enough to allow her heart to express its feelings.

The boy's name was Vaibhav, and the two used to talk often in the class. Naturally, emotions started to seep into the heart, numbing the mind and its associates. With each day passing, the two started experiencing a feeling of fondness for each other.

Gradually, a month went by, and Anvi was officially asked out by Vaibhav during school time as all the friends watched. You had to be there to witness the awesome moment—the first proposal for a girl.

The proposal took Anvi by surprise because she knew the consequences. The news of the proposal quickly spread through the entire grade and reached Anurag, who also studied in the same school. It did not take much time for Shivam and, consequently, Raghavendra to learn of the romantic developments in Anvi's life.

She was unaware of the fact that the news had reached Raghavendra and soon was confronted by an angry father who failed to understand what his young daughter felt and made a decision that would scar Anvi for life.

Parents complain when their children lose affection for them. They forget that their treatment of their child when they are young and vulnerable will take a humongous place in their vengeful hearts, craving freedom from the slave-master relationship.

"What is this new shit I'm hearing of, Anvi? You were proposed to by a boy, and instead of caring about the money and efforts I've been pouring into sustaining your education, you are busy enjoying the company of a boyfriend," Raghavendra said in a voice that would send fear into the spines of his young daughter.

"I didn't accept his proposal, Papa," said Anvi.

"You've lost the right to call me your father. I'm not related to a lustful brat like you. You've disappointed me, and here I thought that you were finally learning the ways of a diligent student. No boy reaches out to a girl out of the blue. You must have sent him signals of your availability," Raghavendra said.

Anvi went silent because she knew that there were feelings in her stomach too, but she did not act on them due to her heart being shackled to her father's wishes. She also knew that whatever explanation she would give, Raghavendra would do what he had decided the first time he heard the news.

"I know the perfect resolution for you," Raghavendra said while grabbing Anvi's hands and taking her to the store room. "This is where you'll stay for the next few weeks, and I'll send a medical application to your school stating that you won't be coming in for the next thirty days."

Raghavendra had his lunch and then went back to his office.

Anvi accepted her fate because she knew tears wouldn't help induce affection in a Thakur. Inclosed in a cube that barely had any space, Anvi broke down, cursing her heart and her mind. The walls in the room were close enough to feel the little girl's pain as her sobbing echoed in the windowless room.

There was barely any space to accommodate the already existing table and chair. The cobwebs came straight out of a horror movie, and the single light in the room won't work. It was hell, and Anvi decided to knock on the door a few minutes later, only to be ignored by the others in the house.

"Let me out; I need to pee," Anvi shouted. "I feel hungry! Mom? *Didi?*"

Nobody came to Anvi's aid and she sat down by the door. As the clock marched forward, the sun also bid adieu, and she took a nap on the filthy mattress that made a weird noise when someone put too much weight on it.

Raghavendra came back later in the night, asking his wife to open Anvi's door, let her relieve herself, and then lock her up again until she came back into her senses.

"Give her all the books she needs for the board exams. Only open the door when she needs to go to the washroom or to fill her stomach; no need to talk to her," Raghavendra ordered Aarti.

The following weeks were hell for Anvi, battling mosquitoes that wanted the taste of her blood in a hellish room as she craved any motion at all.

While Raghavendra thought that his daughter would be able to focus on her studies, things didn't pan out that way. Each day, Anvi used to wait for the night so that she could sleep off her troubles, but the room didn't have a proper bed where she could rest her eyes.

Constantly looking at books is not studying, but often parents fail to understand that part. Well, weeks passed, and Anvi was allowed to come out of her room, her eyes red. With bags under her eyes, she was more like a walking corpse.

"The day after tomorrow is your first exam; don't forget to do well," Aarti said. "Before leaving for the exam each day, I'll be giving you curd; it is considered auspicious in my family."

Fast forward: the exams were over, and when the result came, Anvi performed poorly. Everybody knew what would follow.

When Raghavendra got wind of Anvi's poor grades, he immediately took out his belt but was stopped in his shoes by the wife—the only time Anvi remembered her mother going against her husband.

However, the entire holiday prior to 11th grade, Anvi was locked up in the storeroom, being sucked off any and all emotions.

She didn't feel happy, sad, lonely, or anxious—it was all just a big question mark for her, i.e., until she left for the city.

***

"If you continue to think so hard and reminisce about the bad things in your life, you might get a cardiac arrest one fine day," Apurva turned to Anvi and said. "In the past few years, the cases of heart failure have increased, you know, and you seem like the perfect candidate for it."

"Yeah, well, I kind of don't care anymore. Everyone is just messed up. What happened to the joy in life?" Anvi questioned.

"The gaiety is still there; you're just too invested in the stuff that has already happened. I once had a fling with a guy who left India a year ago. He used to say that life is like pouring whiskey into your glass; the more you pour, the more you won't feel shit. So, keep yourself busy with whiskey, and all your problems will vanish," Apurva advised.

The two girls reached home totally intoxicated and in a bad mood. Apurva, too, had her shit to deal with, but she was never stuck in what had already happened. It has always been her philosophy to focus on the present.

Coming from a poor family and living with restrictions, Apurva learned that hiding things from parents is a gift that girls need to learn with time. While the world might not be safe for women, under the excessive limitations imposed by parents, daughters have to learn how to deal with the world themselves.

"Oh shit, it's already 1 AM; I forgot to call my parents," Apurva said. "Now they'll eat my head. Speaking of parents, don't you call your mother every night to tell her you've had dinner and are praying to God every day?"

"Yeah, well, I told her that I'd sleep all day today. It doesn't matter. I'm going to go and get changed, and you can stay with me tonight," Anvi said.

"You know, I really liked that guy—what was his name? Um, yeah, Ravi! I think I'm going to call him back tomorrow," Apurva said.

"That is just the liquor talking. We both know you're going to ghost him anyway," Anvi replied.

"You know what? I'll text him right now! I don't have commitment issues," Apurva boldly said.

"Well then, what are you going to text him? It was hot making out with you in the smoking room, and you are a good kisser, but we might not meet again," Anvi said it with a sarcastic smile.

"Shut up!" Apurva said this while picking up her phone and opening the messaging application.

Apurva started typing something on her phone while Apurva went inside to put on her go-to pajamas and T-shirt.

A few minutes later, Anvi emerged from the washroom.

"You know, the first thing I did when I came to the city was to get a boyfriend, just to experience what it felt like. To be honest, it's not worth it. Men might seem grown-up, but they are always looking for someone to heal them. I don't really understand what they need healing from. They have an easy and unristricted life, doing whatever they want," Anvi said.

On the other hand, Apurva was already asleep, her phone landing on her forehead. Anvi laughed, immediately capturing the moment via her smartphone.

She removed the phone from Apurva's forehead, treading carefully so as not to disturb the sleeping beauty.

Anvi also decided to enter the bed, covering herself with a blanket, and decided to doze off. All of a sudden, her phone rang—it was Aarti's call.

The first time, Anvi decided to let the call run itself out so that her mother thought that she had gone to bed. Nevertheless, the phone rang once again, and for a third time as well.

The fourth time, Anvi picked up the call and, in a sleepy voice, asked her mother why she was calling so late.

Aarti was silent, but it seemed like she had been sobbing for a while. She was trying to say something, but the words wouldn't come from her mouth.

"What happened, Ma? Is everything okay?" A worried Anvi questioned.

Aarti was unable to speak, as if her tongue were caught in a wire. Mahendra took the phone from her hand and, in a sad voice, broke the news to Anvi.

"Your father passed away."

"What?" Anvi shouted, waking up Apurva.

"He had a heart attack after dinner, and after battling in the hospital for a few hours, he left us," Mahendra confirmed.

"Please tell her to come as soon as possible," Aarti said.

"Your mother didn't want to trouble her daughters initially, but after *Bhaiya* gave up on his life, she had no choice. We have informed Jhanvi as well," Mahendra said.

"I'm coming tomorrow!" Anvi said she was unable to process what she had just heard.

The call was cut.

"What happened?" Apurva asked.

"My father... is dead," Anvi replied with a pause.

"How can he leave us?" Anvi said, breaking down for the man that she hated so much.

Tears poured down her face as she tried to process her feelings.

"I wanted so many answers from him! How could he lock her daughter in a room for months? How could he deprive me of my freedom? Why did he leave without answering all my questions?" Anvi told Apurva.

Apurva hugged Anvi as she cried all night, waiting for the sun to come up so she could go back to the place considered the worst part of her life.

As the morning arrived, Anvi got ready to leave, handing the keys to her friend.

"Sometimes, life tests us; it breaks us down; it doesn't give us the closure we so desperately need; and maybe some questions were never meant to be answered; maybe you are now freed and freedom demands sacrifice," Apurva said.

CHAPTER SIX

PARTING WAYS

Death always leaves with unanswered questions and unfulfilled expectations, with only a treasure trove of moments to knit-pick the memories that one carries to the grave or gets burned with.

Anvi stood on the balcony of the empty house, smoking a cigarette—the only way she knew how to cope with the pain. With each inhale, she felt heavier, not lighter. A heavy and confused heart can fuck you up in innumerable ways.

Seconds later, the cigarette showed signs of dying, and Anvi was annoyed.

"Even you can't last long, can you?" Anvi spoke out loud with no one to hear her.

She threw the cigarette butt, and it landed on a branch of a young tree that her father had planted a few years ago.

"What are the chances of that, huh?" Anvi thought to herself.

The smoke coming out of the butt gradually faded, and all that remained was a yellow-stained object with no tomorrow and no utility.

While standing on the balcony, Anvi wondered why she wasn't getting emotional like her sister and mother, who had gone to Mahendra's, for they couldn't bear to breathe in Raghavendra's house.

"A clueless person is destined for confusion," Anvi thought to herself.

As the smoke cleared, Anvi went inside, opening the fridge, searching for snacks, and stuffing her mouth with whatever she could find.

She dragged the chair where her father used to sit for dinners and claimed it. Moments later, Anvi felt thirsty and stood up to bring her father's tall glass that he used to drink water in.

"It stings, doesn't it, father?" Anvi said.

"Now that you're not here anymore, I wonder if you're getting preferential treatment up there. There was no need for the shit you put everyone through, and things could've been a lot easier, you know?" Anvi said it out loud with a heavy throat.

Anvi once again stood up, and this time she walked towards a large, framed picture of her father that had seamlessly captured Raghavendra's pride.

"It was always a pleasure watching you look at yourself while holding the damn whiskey glass at night. How can a man be obsessed with himself to such an extent that he would fuck up his daughter in the process?" Anvi questioned.

"You were always a pain in the butt and you know, I'm glad you're gone. I won't have to see you again or bear your taunts. The last time I saw you alive, you were up on the balcony, watching me leave with proud eyes. What was that all about? Were you really proud of your daughter leaving for the city where you will never be treated as the Thakur you are? For your information, I don't care anymore if you were proud of me or not," Anvi said while standing next to her father's painting.

She turned her back on the picture and decided to move back to the chair. However, she retraced her steps, and her heart was fuming with anger.

"It would've been nice to hear you say that you were proud of me at least once! Mom always used to say that you loved me dearly, but I never saw that. Were you too proud to even show your love to me? What was wrong with you? What pride did you have when you were burned to ashes, huh? Hell, you were lying with your eyes closed, and all your brothers and their sons got to see you burn today, and here I am, at home, questioning all the things you've done to me in your life," Anvi cursed her father.

Once again, Anvi broke down, sobbing over a person who doesn't exist anymore and is now reduced to dust.

Since when did dust have emotions? Since when did death warn its victims with its steps? Since when did human tears hold any value in the grand scale of events?

***

While Anvi was on the ground, unable to process her emotions, the bell rang. She composed herself and opened it to find Mahendra's wife, her mother, and her sister whispering something about Aarti's future.

"So it has been decided, then?" Aarti asked.

"What?" a puzzled Anvi questioned.

"Well, the three of us have decided that Aarti will be living with us and selling this house. The money we get will be used for Aarti's care and marrying off Jhanvi next year, and then it'll be your turn," Mahendra's wife said.

"What the hell? Who are you to decide this?" Anvi asked.

"Your father is no more. I don't want any more complications in life, and Lord Krishna is my only savior now. So, Mahendra Uncle has already talked to someone who's interested in marrying Jhanvi, and after that, we'll be looking for a husband for you. I don't want any surprises!" Aarti said this while marching towards the kitchen.

"Are you okay with this?" Anvi asked her sister.

"Father is no longer around, so what mom says will happen," Jhanvi said.

"What about the boy you've been seeing?" Anvi asked.

"I've already ended things with him prior to coming here. I had accepted in my heart that this is what destiny wants from me," Jhanvi said as she left for the kitchen as well.

"The fuck is happening here," Anvi thought to herself.

Conversations continued about the future of the girls and Aarti, with sudden outbursts from Jhanvi and her mother. Anvi knew she had no power here, and the struggle was futile. All she could do was try not to end up like her sister.

"I have a job, and I would definitely like to continue it," Anvi exclaimed.

"How much do they pay you? We'll find a rich husband for you to quell your thirst for money. Plus, your father has invested enough that you don't need to stress much," Mahendra's wife said.

"I don't care; I'll be leaving for the city when my leave ends," Anvi said.

"In that case, don't bother coming back," Aarti replied while shedding a few tears.

Anvi left the conversation, going outside to take a break from the anxious talk. She knew that Mahendra's wife was pushing Aarti to get the two sisters married just for the fun of it.

"It'll probably be Anurag—the person they'll choose as my husband," Anvi thought.

She kept walking in the garden, where her father used to spend most of his mornings. It was calm and peaceful, and the cold winds coalesced with the setting sun, painting a sorrowful picture in Anvi's mind as she continued to walk around.

"There it is!" Anvi said this while looking at the table and chair that her father used to sit on every morning.

There was his pen and diary, where he used to note the daily expenses every morning while cursing his family for the rising numbers.

"A few days ago, you'd be seated here, wouldn't you? Like every day, unbothered about the fact that you'd die not much long after," Anvi thought while sitting on the chair.

She picked up Raghavendra's diary, turning pages one-by-one to find all the calculations that he used to do every morning. The entries ended abruptly, and a few pages later, Anvi found out that her father liked to write.

"What the.....?" Anvi said.

I wonder, what if I cease to exist,
What if I vanish and do not resist?
I wonder if the absence of water droplets on the grass,
Would it affect the relations I've built with glass?
I wonder if the fabric of my being ends here,
Would I even care?
I wonder if I won't see the sun tomorrow,
Would my eyes gleam in sorrow?
What would happen if I were no more,
Would I still think about the things I abhor?
I wonder, what if I cease to exist,
Deep down, do I crave the easy exit?"

This was the last poem that Raghavendra wrote. Anvi continued to turn the pages to find more, but all she could find were calculations.

"Where would I find more?" Anvi thought to herself.

She immediately rushed to her father's study room, avoiding the calls of her aunt and mother. Anvi opened the drawers of Raghavendra's desk that no one dared to come close to.

There were three drawers, one on top of the other. The first two had nothing useful, and the third one wouldn't open.

Anvi tried hard to open the drawer but could not. There was a lock that guarded the material inside.

"Smart work wins!" Anvi exclaimed and removed the top two drawers completely, exposing the material in the bottom drawer to the intruder.

There were pages of poems and lines that Raghavendra had written, describing something called "pain running in the family."

"There is a strange pain that runs through my family,

I fear for you, Anvi:

For you resemble me.

I carry a curse of unbearable pain,

I kept out of your life because I didn't want you to go insane.

I do care for you, your sister, and your mother, but I can't show it,

All I can do is write my emotions, bit-by-bit."

The abundance of emotions that Raghavendra had never shown were all penned down, and Anvi's heart was too fragile to manage them.

She immediately took whatever material she could and hid the pages beneath her dress, running off to her room.

***

Comprehensive thoughts bother the heart due to emotional exhaustion, and feelings, when disturbed, place unnecessary weight on the soul.

Anvi, locked inside her room, was robbed of all certainty in her mind, and confusion prevailed. She questioned the existence of this 'curse' and what Raghavendra meant by the poems he wrote.

She also found a small diary that her mind knew she shouldn't read, but her heart could not resist.

"I was overjoyed when I saw my first daughter come out of her mother's womb," were the first words that Raghavendra wrote in the diary. "It felt like this curse of sadness was finally over with me, but I couldn't have been more wrong."

"As I watched my second daughter grow, I realized that the curse had found its way to her. I tried to push myself away from my young daughter so she wouldn't take on me, but I failed," Raghavendra further added.

The diary contained the words of a man who hid behind his pride to protect his feeble heart. Anvi decided to close the diary after going through the first few statements. It was too much for her young mind to handle.

She wondered if Aarti knew that her husband liked to write. Naturally, Anvi's instincts asked her to question her mother, but she realized that it would do more harm than good for Aarti.

Anvi decided to come out of her room and hide the pages and the diary with her paintings. Maybe art is the luxury that only cursed and broken hearts can afford.

Mahendra and others were already downstairs, talking about the cremation and how the feast would be thrown the next day to celebrate Raghavendra's life.

Anvi remembered how, back when she was a kid, she used to ask her father about death and what happened after.

"When I close my eyes, I only see darkness. Will I see the same thing when I die, Papa?" A young daughter asked her father.

"Death is a complex celebration, and there is no opening of eyes after that. You can only hope that there is an afterlife, but what my father told me is that once a person is gone, the only thing they leave are the consequences of their decisions and the relationships they have made. He used to say that death is inevitable, so why not die a proud death? Well, you're too young for these questions; maybe focus more on studies instead of drawings," Raghavendra replied.

Anvi ran downstairs and immediately asked Mahendra about the curse that Raghavendra mentioned in the notes.

"Since you're going to celebrate my father's life, do you know about this 'family curse' because he mentioned it to me a few times earlier this year?" Anvi asked Mahendra.

"That was some rubbish that our father used to repeat on his deathbed. Raghavendra *Bhaiya* spent the most time on his side, so he must've mentioned it to you while talking about *Dadaji's* death. Father used to say that one person in our lineage is always cursed with sadness and an acute sense of detachment after a certain age. I guess his mind was rotten after the accident, and Raghavendra *Bhaiya* took his blabber seriously," said Mahendra.

Anvi knew that this wasn't the closure she needed.

"Well, why are you asking such questions? I will reiterate the fact that I've been telling your mother since *Bhaiya* left us—there is no meaning to death. Don't try to attach one," Mahendra said.

"It was just a question that popped into my mind today, you know? I never got to really understand what went inside my father's prideful mind," Anvi replied.

"Well, no one knows what goes inside the mind of anyone because our mind is constantly exposed to different opinions and thoughts. So, it's futile to run after uncertain things. Well, talking about certain things, your mother has decided that she'd like to get you married after Jhanvi," Mahendra said.

"Let me guess, Anurag." Anvi replied.

"Well, he's an ideal candidate. He is of the same cast and is well-off. I won't impose this decision on you, but I'd definitely like you to consider him. He has liked you for quite a long time and could be your knight in shining armor," Mahendra suggested.

"Hmm, give me some time, and I will answer your question before my leave ends," Anvi replied.

"I'm sure you know that you are not going back to the city. I seriously advise you to not go against your mother's wishes. Take care of her as your father is no more, and Jhanvi will also be getting married in the near future," Mahendra said.

"Like I said, give me some time; you'll have your answer soon," Anvi said.

She went back to her room to read her father's belongings further. The unanswered questions were eating her away as each second passed by.

Maybe she felt that the pages were Raghavendra's way of talking to her from beyond the grave and answering her questions. It is never easy to accept death, and people often try to attach meaning to it.

However, the fact that has stood the test of time is that death never had a meaning. It has come to everyone who has inhaled the air on this land and will continue to lurk around every nook and cranny until one's luck has been exhausted.

Anvi took out one of the pages on which Raghavendra wrote:

"Oh, how fast time flies!
One minute you see your first daughter getting born,
The next few years seem like lies.
Oh, how fast the time goes by!
One minute you're getting married,
The next few years, you want to erase the curse, you try—
To create a new you,
To refrain from saying goodbye.
Oh, how fast the time marches on!
One minute you live for your pride,
The next few years, you're gone!"

CHAPTER SEVEN

THE CURSE

"A curse flows through my family," Raghavendra wrote in his small diary. "My father and his father before, we are all cursed with pride, sadness, detachment, contemplation, and the nimbleness of the heart."

A new morning dawned, and Anvi was up earlier than usual, pushing through the pages of Raghavendra's small diary.

"My grandfather was a government official, but a brutally honest one. He never took bribes, and by the time my father was born, his family was already struggling to make ends meet. When my father got older, he got the job at the same office as my grandfather but at a very junior rank. He failed to earn much in terms of salary, but what he had learned from his father was to always take bribes—he took 'em. However, we were still not very rich, and my brothers looked up to me, as did my only sister," Raghavendra continued.

"I messed up during the early stages of life, and despite my father trying to get me a good education, I failed to catch up. I was never a good student, but I needed money by the time I was an adolescent. I started flipping through notebooks that my father bought for me. If he bought one for 2 rupees, I'd sell it for 4 and blow the money on cigarettes and other shit," he wrote.

Anvi was confused. She never knew that her father had a notorious side and was a delinquent.

"The shit went on and on for a year as I continued to demand more notebooks from my father. He was suspicious and somehow got hold of the fact that I was selling the notebooks. That was the first time my father hit me, and I was bruised from head to toe. He was sad, and it felt like I would never be able to make him proud. I tried very hard but failed every time, and that is when the sadness crept up in my life," the diary read.

"How come you hid all this stuff over the years, you idiot?" Anvi thought to herself.

"Well, I started filling the notebooks, each notebook with one single question repeated over and over again just to get back at my father. I remember once I hit the son of a policeman, and I came home, afraid, not going out for days. He sensed something was wrong and asked me why I wasn't out doing my thing. I told him and expected a heavy beatdown, but he laughed and said that he knew the Commissioner and nothing would happen. For a young adult, that was enough to instill confidence and break the fear of not going out. I realized that he might be lying about having relations with the Commissioner, but his words made me feel like someone had my back," Raghavendra wrote.

"Anvi!" Aarti shouted, calling her daughter's name. "Help us out here!"

"Coming," Anvi replied from inside her room, once again closing the diary and hiding it in a safe place.

Anvi came outside the room looking like she hadn't slept all night, which was indeed true.

"We are looking for potential suitors for your sister, and we need your input as well," Aarti said.

"For God's sake, father just passed away, and you're already planning to move on," Anvi retorted.

The words hurt her mother, who immediately started sobbing.

"Moving on is a part of life. We all can't be stuck here forever. I don't want her to constantly hear your harsh words all her life, so just take your tone to your will-be husband. Anurag's out here waiting and wants to talk to you," Mahendra's wife chimed in.

"What?" Anvi said while moving towards the door and going outside.

Anurag was standing outside, a little nervous and hesitant but excited nonetheless. While men might be simple creatures, they can be selfish as well.

He knew that Anvi would finally cave in to the pressure created by Mahendra, his wife, and Aarti and would have to accept him as her husband.

"Here," Anurag said while handing Anvi a bunch of roses tied together.

"You know, mister, you've gone to great lengths to only get rejected," Anvi said. "You don't take advantage of a situation and try to win a girl you like. Life doesn't work that way."

"Anvi, listen to me. You have to settle down now. The city has corrupted your mind, don't you see? I have everything you'd ever need, and I can even keep you comfortable financially. Why do you have to be so difficult? You're not going back; there is no career for you. After all, Raghavendra Uncle would've wanted the same. He wasn't ever expecting you to become a big-shot architect," Anurag said.

These words from Anurag hurt Anvi, and the anger that she felt could burn down Hell. However, she maintained her composure, stating:

"I will talk to you once I have my answer. My leave ends in two days, and you will have the closure you need."

"Explain yourself whatever you want, Anvi. There is no other way, and this is it. We all have to give up sometimes and accept our fate. I could never become a musician like I always wanted to. Dreams are only for those with no responsibilities, no care, and no need for money. Me and you? We don't have the courage to put it all on the line," Anurag said.

Anvi gave a cold smile and started going inside, turning her back on Anurag, who thought that he had won the battle and now Anvi would be his.

"What the fuck do you even want?" Anurag shouted.

Anvi kept going forward, contemplating and debating her own thoughts.

***

"When I gave the exams for the government jobs, all the questions that I had so far repeatedly scribbled in my notebooks helped me clear the papers in the first attempt. It was a miracle, and I will always be indebted to my father for that. I had a period of six months before I could join the job, and during that period, my sister was due to be married. While coming from a car after booking the marriage venue, he met with an accident, and everything fell on my shoulders. His health only deteriorated after this moment, but I kept at his side, and with the help of the donations from the relationships he earned over the years, I successfully married off my sister," Raghavendra continued.

"Okay," Anvi thought to herself.

"The curse took a stronghold in my mind once my father died without answering my questions. Did he know that being hard on me all my life would turn me into a successful person? I have everything in my life today, but I really feel empty, so I write what I feel in this diary that will only be discovered once I'm gone. Should I be hard on Anvi knowing that she carries the curse?" The diary further read.

The next few pages went blank again, and it seemed like Raghavendra stopped writing after the death of his father.

Anvi kept on turning the pages, finally finding an entry.

"Today, I hit Anvi and cut down her hair because a boy was messing with her. I feel bad, but I had to do it. She can't be behaving like this because I need to keep my father's name proud. I can't tarnish his image, for he was a great man, respected everywhere. If Anvi continues to indulge in notoriety, my name will be dragged through the mud, and my father's lineage will be hurt," Raghavendra wrote.

Anvi could sense the change in her father's words and understanding after the latest entry she read. Something flipped his mind, changing his identity.

"I guess this 'curse' was just a way to justify your behavior towards your children; isn't it father? Your father talked about this curse to you, and instead of changing yourself, you decided to carry this bullshit on for years and take it out on me. I am not 'cursed' for I am not from your 'respected lineage.' I am just a normal human—a being still trying to figure out if her father loved her or hated the idea of her existence," Anvi said while holding onto the little diary.

The diary was finished, and no more entries were to be found, except the one Raghavendra wrote after Anvi left his house the last time.

"I am writing this while watching my daughter leave. I feel that I've let her down, and I probably won't be able to look her in the eye ever again. I guess my curse cost me my beautiful daughter, and she'll probably resent me throughout her life. I never wanted this to happen, but I guess I just repeated my father's mistakes," read the last few words in the diary.

"All my accomplishments seem worthless. Like my father, I craved respect from the outside world and my family, and in turn, I respected everyone else other than the three people that have always been close to me. This 'curse' led me to a road where the end is undesirable but the journey is poisonous," Raghavendra penned down.

"One last thing I would say to you, Anvi," Raghavendra said. "Please be free of this curse. My father told me on his deathbed, but I failed, and now I lay this burden on you. Please be free and don't pass it on. It should end with you. Don't listen to anyone; run away from my influence, my reach, and my possessions. Figure out what you want to be and just be free."

***

Nobody knows the perfect road through life or the ideal way of upbringing. One can only learn from the mistakes they have made through the journey and try not to push through the stop sign at the edge of the road.

Anvi got up from the bed, gathered all of Raghavendra's belongings, and placed them on her table, which was already covered with a lot of dust.

She didn't feel anything except a rage that sent chills down her spine and brought her ears to a fumingly hot temperature. She picked up the possessions and went downstairs to the storage room.

She sat in the storage room on the filthy mattress that had been placed there when Anvi was locked inside it. Anvi kept the diary and other pages in front of her, continuously staring at them, aiming to grasp what her father wanted to say.

"It was you, wasn't it, who never wanted me to be with any man, never wanted me to go out with friends, or even have a sip of a sweet beverage until I'd earned it by pleasing you? Now, you want me to be fucking free? Free of fucking what? You want me to do the shit you were supposed to do, huh? You arrogant bastard! I hate you! Who do you think you are, you inconsiderate moron? Was everything just an experiment for you? When I was weak, all I had was you. I thought I could trust you, and meanwhile, you were blaming your incapability on a fucking 'curse.' Where is your pride now?" An agitated Anvi, intoxicated with rage, said.

"You ruined my life!" Anvi shouted, breaking down, sobbing profusely, and letting her emotions out of her heart. "How can I ever get back at you? You're not even here anymore! I wish you were alive so I could kill you again, you.....ugh!"

Half an hour passed by, and Mahendra and others were completely oblivious to what was happening in the storage room, possibly because they were discussing the division of estates and marriage of Aarti's daughters.

Anvi had fallen asleep after her anger subsided. She woke up ten minutes later, brushed off the dust on her clothes, and immediately picked up all her father's possessions.

"You know what you deserve, you monster," Anvi said while looking at the diary and the pages.

She picked up a jar that was used to bring water to her when she was locked up. She then left the storage room, sneaking into the nearest bathroom to fill the jar with water. She came back to the room and immediately closed the door behind her.

Anvi picked up the pages, tore them to shreds, stuffed everything, leaving just the small diary, into the mouth of the jar, and closed it with the lid.

She looked around the room and finally hid the diary in a hole in the wall, which she had made back when she was locked, just out of boredom.

She closed off the hole with another container, locked the storage room with its key, and ran outside.

"Anvi! Where are you going?" Mahendra questioned her as she opened the door.

"I'm just going to get some air," Anvi replied.

"Okay! I hope you have thought about my proposal," Mahendra asked.

"Well, I guess I don't have any choice. So, let's take the marriage proposal to Anurag's house tomorrow at 11 a.m. and I'll get married by the end of the year, I promise," Anvi said.

"Perfect! I'm proud of you. Look at you maturing," Mahendra noted.

Anvi smiled and moved across the garden to open the gates of the house. She stood on the road, searching for a particular place where she could get rid of the jar and the key.

She walked for a few minutes and found sewage construction work being done in the area. Anvi snuck near the site and just threw the jar and the key when no one was around, walking off casually back towards the house, experiencing a rush of adrenaline in her heart.

"How fun was that?" Anvi thought to herself. "Take that, Raghavendra Singh. This is where your pride and your 'curse' led you, in a fucking sewer!"

CHAPTER EIGHT

5 PAISE

Mountains mean freedom for many—freedom from nice things, from negative emotions, from other people, and often from loneliness.

The birds that run in patterns, the cold breeze that warms the heart, the clean water that purifies the emotions, and the clouds kissing the cheeks can all be mesmerizing and overwhelming.

While the quiet and peace might work as escapance for many, there are chances that a broken heart might further crumble into pieces at inundating altitudes.

"So, how did you manage to escape?" Apurva asked Anvi.

"Well, I gathered my things, snuck out in the night, went to the bus station, took the bus to the city, and the next thing I remember is sleeping in my rented apartment," Anvi replied.

"I never expected you to return. I thought you'd get married off and contact me when you'd give birth to your first child," Apurva mocked.

"Um, I gave you the first call after arriving in the morning, didn't I? Also, for fuck's sake, give me a little credit. I'm the one who planned this trip to Mussoorie so that my uncle wouldn't be able to force me to go back because he knows my address back in the city," Anvi said.

"If you don't mind me asking, how was it? Losing your father can result in a mental beatdown. Anything you'd like to share?" Apurva questioned.

"Now, if I wanted to deal with that stuff, I wouldn't be going to a hill station, you idiot. I want to experience peace for a day or two; maybe enjoy the clean air and release some of my baggage," Anvi said.

"Or maybe meet some boys?" Apurva interrupted.

"Haha, very funny, joker!" Anvi said while being seemingly annoyed. "I'm not looking for relationships, and you and the others need to understand that shit. I like boys at a distance, you can say. *Mai kaat turant deti hun, sochti baad mei hun* (I break hearts first and then think about what I did)," Anvi replied.

The taxi driver was gradually picking up the pace as the curvy roads and blind turns in the mountains gave him a sudden sense of excitement. He would rotate the car to the left and right while the people sitting in the vehicles would follow, grabbing anything that would make them remain seated.

As the elevation gradually started rising, Anvi and Apurva's ears closed up.

"Hey! Do you feel something weird in your ear?" Apurva asked Anvi.

"I guess this happens at higher altitudes?" She replied.

Anvi and Apurva heard strange sounds of vehicles coming in hot and looked out the window to see a barrage of motorcycle enthusiasts pass them by swiftly, waving at the two of them.

"What do they think of themselves? I mean, their loud ass machines and heavily armored bodies are a disturbing sight to see," Apurva said. "These are death machines; one fall and all that expensive shit goes down the drain."

"I don't know; I like motorcycles," Anvi replied.

"I can't seem to get a grasp on your personality, bitch," Apurva added.

"These motorcycle enthusiasts seek to achieve freedom through speed, but at the end of the day, it is temporary, but nothing ever lasts, does it? Momentary happiness might be short-lived, but it's pleasant," Anvi said.

"Dude, what the fuck happened to you back home? All of a sudden, the idiot that ran away from a date is now giving me life lessons," Apurva said with a strong laugh.

The taxi suddenly stopped near a tea shop.

"Anyone who'd like to have some tea can do so because I'll be stopping here for only ten minutes," said the driver.

There were a total of six people in the taxi, and four of them got out immediately.

"Should we get out as well?" Apurva asked.

"Sure, let's smoke a cigarette and buy a few for when we land at the hostel," Anvi replied.

The duo got out of the car and purchased a few packets. Anvi lit up one, and the two shared, not saying a single word but embracing the beauty of the landscape.

The tea shop was standing at the edge of a cliff, and looking down, Anvi could see how small the world was when seen from the height where she was standing.

The cars in the distance, the schools, the buildings, and the people all seemed like ants working in a colony without a goal. The rush of the city, the dirt from the construction, the impatience at traffic stops, and the stupidity of the people all seemed so confined in a circle called the city.

Anvi inhaled the smoke, letting the brief moment of numbness take control, and passed the cigarette to Apurva.

"This is nice. I like it here," Apurva said.

"Do you like this place, or do you like the person who you are at this place?" Said an old person, wearing nothing on his body, as if the cold didn't bother him.

Anvi and Apurva were startled by the sudden interest shown by the sage in their conversation. The two were scared and immediately started moving away from the man. His naked body didn't serve his cause either.

"Won't you give this old soul 5 paise?" The sage begged.

"We don't have any money," Anvi said.

"We are both just students," Apurva said, backing her friend.

The duo was alarmed and immediately started making their way towards the taxi.

"I just want 5 paise, nothing else," said the sage.

Apurva hesitatingly took out her purse and gave the sage a 10 rupee note, asking him to leave the two alone.

"Huh," said the sage while throwing the currency on the ground and crushing it with his legs.

"You don't understand, do you? Your losses are piling up," he said while looking at Anvi and walking away singing a melodious song, the meaning of which only he understood:

"What if I told you, I hang out with God every day?

Well, you won't believe me anyway.

I met with God and asked Him what's the purpose of my breath,

I asked him, what's beyond death?

You see, I wanted to know what's going on with me,

I sought to know where the questions and answers meet.

I was having rest in the night, killing time in the day,

Like most people, I didn't care about God anyway.

I wanted to know why I never liked hanging around others,

Why was I unable to walk the path I was directed to?
Was that because I'm dear to You?
Well, of course, He said everything is predestined,
But why does He give us the tools to change our destiny?
Hearing my questions potentially, God replied:
'I am the moon and the Sun,
I am the infinite and the one.
I am the ignorant and the enlightened,
I am both brave and frightened.
I am the successful and the failed:
I am the good and the bad,
Don't curse me, and stay mad.
You see:
It's your choice; I've given you all the tools,
You are the one who has decided to remain fools.'"

***

"What was that all about?" Apurva asked Anvi.

"God. A pretty stereotypical example of unlimited power. Once a human created a perfect entity that he wanted to be but was never able to be," Anvi replied.

Everyone got in the vehicle. Anvi and Apurva tried to make their peers jealous by repeatedly posting photos on social media they captured by extending their arms outside the taxi's window.

"Take care; we wouldn't want your phone to fall off," Apurva warned Anvi. "We don't have the budget to buy a new one."

"I wish I had the budget; I'm constantly getting calls from relatives that I'm avoiding!" Anvi replied.

The two arrived at a hostel, a humongous property constructed around a stream that originated in the mountains above and fell down, regulating the flow, so that the guests on the property could enjoy their stay near a calm source of water.

There is something in the sound that constantly flowing water makes—the waves beating the land and the rocks, the small fish trying to make its way towards food—the overwhelming silence can be hypnotic.

It was almost night, and the entire place was lit up like it was Christmas or Diwali. The place was completely filled with tourists who wanted to stay far from the luxurious crowd of Mussoorie and enjoy the silence of the mountains while making new friends.

Anvi and Apurva got off the taxi, paying the driver off and bidding adieu. The duo started walking to the hostel, which was visible but somewhat far.

"I hate walking!" Apurva said.

"Who doesn't?" Anvi said.

Meanwhile, two dogs interrupted their conversation, wagging their tails as if asking to escort the young females.

Both were furry with big eyes and curved tails, which Anvi tried to straighten only for it to return to their original stature.

Anvi has loved dogs since she was young and even tried convincing her father to get one for her, only to be shut down.

"You know, I always wanted two dogs and even thought of their names—Johnny and Manny," she said.

"Let's name the brown one Johnny and the white one Manny—although to me it looks like a girl, haha," said a chuckling Apurva.

Anvi felt a cold breeze running through her back and immediately brought out the overcoat she had borrowed from Apurva back in the city and covered her head with a beanie, struggling with her hair and trying to get it in place.

The two continued to walk towards the hostel and gave up a few minutes into the walk, tired of carrying the heavy bags that they stuffed their clothes into.

From the hostel came a man, about Anvi's age, with broad shoulders and ashy lips that seemed to have gotten used to being burned every time they sucked the life out of a cigarette butt.

The guy had a huge beard and was smoking his cigarette, not paying any attention, just moving forward, thinking about something, and possibly engaging in a conversion with himself.

The man continued to come closer while Anvi and Apurva sat on the ground with the dogs, exhausted and tired of the short journey.

"Should we ask this person to help us?" Apurva suggested.

"I don't know," Anvi replied.

Meanwhile, Johnny and Manny suddenly started wagging their tails and immediately ran towards the man, smelling him from hips to legs, trying to tell him that they missed him.

"Woahh, easy," said the man whose cigarette just fell from his hands.

Johnny started jumping in the air, keeping his front paws on the man's chest while standing on his hind legs. He immediately picked up the dog using its body, as if holding a baby, and the dog gave him a few licks on the face as he started laughing.

Anvi felt that she could trust this man and maybe ask him to help them out. Meanwhile, Manny was feeling left and continued to pounce on the man's back to give it a chance as well.

As the man put Johnny down, both dogs ran towards Anvi, who immediately stood up to prevent herself from getting rammed by the two beasts.

The man looked at Anvi, playing with the two dogs, her face redder than a sweet potato, her head covered by a beanie, and the beautiful hair flailing in the air, settling down on her cheeks, creating an enchanting picture in his mind.

Anvi's laugh started to warm his heart, but he refrained from looking further. "Beauty can be treacherous," his mind said. "Especially the beauty that is not on display for others."

Playing with the dogs and giggling like a little girl, it seemed that it was the first time Anvi had laughed in quite a while. The man could see her face glow amid the darkness; his heart was testing the capabilities of his mind.

The smiling face left a lasting impression on this man's feeble, shattered, and exhausted heart. The grace of Anvi's smile seemed to slow the time down for Kathan; he felt like the luckiest person who had just captured the picture of a snow leopard in snow-capped mountains.

"There is something in her; she reminds me of someone. Look at her; she's just so pure, so ugh, just so beguiling," the man thought to himself.

"Kathan! I'm warning you: stop your heart here. I'm not going to play ball with you anymore. Another crack in this castle of glass that you call your heart would be detrimental. You're wrong to think that women can heal you. No one can heal anyone; they can only understand, not feel," the man's inner monologue told him.

"I'm going ahead," Kathan argued to himself.

He couldn't resist the temptation that Anvi's presence had created in his heart. The man could smell the woman's sadness a mile away but was hypnotized by her skill of laughing—a skill that he could never perfect.

On the other hand, Anvi was engrossed in her own world, not knowing that the man whom she was about to meet would fall for her faster than light travels in a dimly lit room. For a moment, the shield that the girl had created around her for years was gone and she felt safer in the moment than she had since childhood.

***

"Hi, those are my dogs, haha! Well, I noticed that you might need some help with the stuff you've been carrying, and to be honest, those bags seem heavy for the two of you," said the man to Anvi.

"Hello! That would be a great help," Apurva said. "I'm Apurva, and she's Anvi, my best friend. We both are aspiring architects."

"I'm Kathan, an aspiring writer," the guy said.

"Well then, writer *Sahab*, nice to meet you, and could you please help us with the bags?" Apurva said.

"Sure, let's go," Kathan replied, and Johnny and Manny followed the trio.

"So, you are here alone?" Anvi questioned, breaking the silence.

"Well, yes. I came here to gather ideas for my book, and after this, I'm going to lock myself in my apartment back in the city and not come out until I get the book done," Kathan confirmed.

"That's great, I guess?" Anvi said.

"Anvi, you seem to have some story on your mind. I am good at reading expressions. So, maybe later on, if you'd like to, I'm all ears," Kathan said.

"Hm," Anvi said.

"I'm telling you, you're going to fuck this shit up too. The person who can't stand to see himself in the mirror would like to write a book on someone else. Nice joke," said Kathan's inner voice.

Not much later, the trio was at the destination, and Kathan parted ways with Anvi and Apurva and went inside one of the dormitories.

Soon after, a staff member entered Kathan's dormitory, showing Anvi and Apurva their beds.

"Well, well, well, it looks like we are going to be friends for the next few days," said Apurva.

"If that's what destiny wants, then why not?" Kathan said.

"How many days are you going to stay here?" Anvi questioned.

"I don't know. Maybe a few? What about you both?" Kathan further asked.

"Well, two at max. We have other places to be as well!" Apurva noted.

"You know what? Before we go to sleep, why don't you read us one of your writings?" Apurva added.

"I don't know; I mean, they can be quite a handful at times!" Kathan said.

"Come on!" Anvi chimed in.

"Well then, here's one," Kathan continued.

"What I want to be,

A short poem by me.

Sometimes, I want to be wealthy,

Sometimes, I want to be healthy.

Sometimes, I don't know where to start,

Sometimes, I want to find courage in my rusty heart.

Sometimes, I feel the continuous urge to travel,

*Sometimes, I want to shut the doors while standing on the
other side with a shovel.
Sometimes, I want to play the piano and the guitar,
Pick up these instruments and be a star.
I want this, and then I want that,
I want to remain bald and not wear a hat.
This is my life, full of contradictions. You see:
I don't know what I want to be."*

KATHAN

When the sun rises in the Himalayas, a purple hue surrounds the sky, and if one gets lucky, they might see birds with violet feathers cross the horizon.

The mountains gradually turn orange, shedding their dark skin, and later in the day, turn green. Throughout the day, the clouds also change their shades, ranging from gray to white and everything in between.

Kathan was up early, watching the clouds gradually pass over his head amid the absence of noise as everyone was asleep. Sitting on his chair, looking up, he tried to peek into the atmosphere, but his gaze wasn't powerful enough to penetrate into the inevitable reality of life.

"What about the girl, Kathan?" his inner voice said.

"What about her? She's a girl, nothing else. They come and go, and if you continue to think about them, your rationality will burn itself to death," Kathan replied.

"Don't you think she's different? She has that aura around her, like she could understand you," the voice said.

"Weren't you the one last night telling me to stay away from her because I'm a fuckup? Why can't you just agree with me for once?" Kathan retorted.

"I mean, think about it! That cute face with the cap—the child in her—might bring out your innocence too. Maybe this is the end to your sadness—maybe this time around, you'll finally get over the weed and alcohol. She could fix you, is what I'm trying to say," the voice argued.

"I don't need fixing. I'm where I was supposed to be. I don't think harrowing over her existence would change things. I know that whenever I'm too close to the things I think I want, they go further away from my grasp. Nothing changes!" Kathan replied.

"Hey! What're you doing up early?" Anvi questioned, shivering out in the cold with sleepy eyes and a messed-up look.

"Well, thinking about you, I guess. Just joking, I have been sitting here since sunrise, watching the colors change in the sky," Kathan said.

"Well, what's your plan for today?" Anvi asked.

"I don't know. Maybe write something, but I don't really have any material to write. You seem like you are hiding some pretty interesting stories," Kathan guessed.

"Nope! I don't," Anvi said, shutting Kathan off.

A moment of silence prevailed as the two sat side by side. Anvi lit up a cigarette, sharing it with Kathan, both looking at the sky, trying to collect the fragments formed from broken emotions inside their individual hearts.

"You know what? You'd look good on a bike," Kathan said. "The day before yesterday, I met another writer. I think his name was Parth. He was on a marvelous bike, traveling alone, talking to everyone here, and collecting stores for a new book he was working on. He said that although girls refrain from motorcycling, the machines look good on a few of them. I guess you'd look cool on one too.

"I know, right? I know my way around a motorcycle. Back when I was a kid, I tried once and fell, and I got a lot of criticism from my father for dropping his beloved. But you know, the following night, he took me for ice cream," Anvi said.

"Your father seems like a complicated man," Kathan said.

"What makes you say that?" Anvi questioned.

"Well, it seemed like it would've been a proud moment for him if you didn't crash the motorcycle, but the fact that you did, he couldn't digest," Kathan said.

"I don't know; he kind of was," Anvi said.

"Was?" Kathan asked.

"Yeah, well, he died a few weeks ago," Anvi said.

"I'm so sorry," Kathan said.

"It's fine! Don't bother," Anvi added.

Another moment of silence prevailed while Kathan took out a cigarette from his pocket and burned it.

The sound of the stream was audible throughout the property, and the two closed their eyes, exchanging the lung dart periodically.

"Say it. Speak up!" Kathan's inner voice demanded.

"You know, in the past few years, I've been through hell and back. It has been an amazing ride, but something tells me that the next few months won't end well for me. My heart continues to sink lower and lower each day," Kathan said.

"Shut up! You are just romanticizing sadness in your mind," Anvi replied. "We all do it. Like you said, sometimes things are in the palm of your hands, but you're unable to grasp them—this feeling of sadness is a consequence of such situations layered on top of each other."

Another cigarette was burned and shared, and another moment of silence prevailed.

"I feel like drinking tonight," Kathan said.

"Same," Anvi replied.

"Partyyy!" Apurva said while barging into the conversation, annoyed that she got woken up by someone flushing the washroom multiple times in a few minutes.

"Yeah, yeah, party," Anvi said.

"It seems like the two of you are getting to know each other a lot, huh?" Apurva said it in a teasing manner.

Kathan laughed it off while walking away from the duo towards the stream, where Johnny was sitting silent, watching the water fall from the mountain above and turn into a stream.

Anvi gave a death stare to Apurva and decided to return inside.

"What?" Apurva questioned herself as she followed Anvi back into the dorm.

"Come here, my boy," Kathan said while grabbing hold of the dog and pushing him to his side, scratching his ears and head.

The man and the animal were engrossed in the peace that the sound of the stream running and the water falling made, while gradually, everyone in the hostel was awake, talking, whispering, and scratching their groins and asses.

"Look at all of these idiots; by the time the sun sets, everyone will be in new clothes, all tidied up, and this place will be like a whorehouse with drunk people flirting with each other, trying to get laid," said Kathan's inner voice.

"Why do you have to be so damn dramatic all the time?" Kathan replied to his own fucking mind.

***

Kathan was out on a walk, while Anvi and Apurva decided to roam around the city a little. The hostel was quiet once again, as every resident had something to do in the afternoon. Some had eaten a lot and slept, while others were engaged in card games.

Slowly, the sun decided to go behind the mountains, creating a semi-dark state for the people on the back side of the mountain. Once again, the skies started changing colors and turned from orange to purple with each hour passing by while the birds decided to go back to their nests, making similar sounds countless times.

Anvi, Apurva, and Kathan found each other once again, walking towards the hostel, tired from spending the entire day on their feet.

"Why don't you give me your number? I was thinking of calling you to ask what type of drink you like, but I didn't have your number, so I just bought a bottle of whiskey," Anvi said.

"Fuck! I already have a bottle of whiskey in my bag," Kathan said while laughing. "Give me your phone; I'll input my digits."

"You both can share one bottle, and I get to drink this one alone," a cheerful Apurva jokingly said. "I wish I had also brought a 'friend' with me."

"Well, I'm going to change into something more comfortable," Anvi said.

"I'm also coming," Apurva said as the duo vanished into the dormitory once again.

"Kathan, keep your composure when you're drunk. I know you drink to silence me, and trust me, it won't be a good idea," the inner voice warned.

"How much worse can life get? After a certain point, it's all a joke," Kathan replied, and he reserved three chairs in front of the stream while taking out a bottle of whiskey from his bag and slamming it softly on the table.

The clock ticked, people came and went, Kathan poured a glass for himself, and then another, and another. He was already feeling a little inebriated but couldn't seem to stop himself—what do you expect from an addict?

"Woah, you already seem drunk," Apurva said, grabbing a chair at the corner, leaving the middle one for Anvi, who sat beside Kathan seconds later.

Everyone poured drinks for themselves as per their need—a scenario that seemed like the three were distributing momentary happiness in glasses.

"Ganbei!" Apurva shouted as the three emptied their glasses simultaneously.

"This deserves a status update!" Apurva said this while capturing the moment on her phone and circulating it via social media.

"Why not?" Kathan said.

Anvi and Kathan had been exchanging stares but were hesitant to speak, despite the liquor warming their hearts. On the other hand, slightly intoxicated, Apurva decided to take a stroll and find a man to talk to.

"You know, you both can continue to have this stare-down competition while I try to score myself a nice piece of ass," Apurva said and walked away, laughing.

"So, you're going to tell me?" Kathan said.

"What?" Anvi questioned.

"What is troubling you?" Kathan asked.

"Nothing!" Anvi said.

"Something is," Kathan replied.

"What do you want to know, *hein*?" An irritated Anvi said.

"The thing that's bothering you," Kathan doubled down on his query.

"I lost my father, okay! He has been an ignorant bastard and an asshole to me his entire life. He had never shown affection or love for me, and yet, after his death, he wrote these meaningless messages, stating that I should free myself from some 'curse,' Anvi said.

"Carry on," Kathan said.

"Well, I can't really remember the last time he hugged me or told me that he's proud of me. One fine day, he decides to just pass away in his sleep. I can't digest this shitty fact," Anvi said while chugging the liquor straight from the bottle.

"He cut off my hair when I was young; he took all the things that made me smile away from me and asked me to alienate myself from all my friends so his pride wouldn't be affected! What kind of man does that?" Anvi questioned.

"To be honest, understanding a parent has never been my cup of tea. I believe that they have been fucked at a deeper level than us, and in an attempt to protect us from that bullshit, they messed up their relationship with their children," Kathan said.

Anvi continued to tell her story while Kathan kept looking at her sorrowful face, which still smiled. The time slowed down, and all he could see were the broken girl's lips moving back and forth, and a sudden feeling of warmth once again promulgated in his heavy heart.

He could see Anvi's hair dropping from behind her ears, and she kept trying to push them back. Kathan gradually brought forth his hand and took the girl's cold hands in his warm palms.

"Well, it doesn't matter now," Anvi said. "He's gone, and I couldn't care less."

"While I can understand your frustration, I don't have a solution for it. You have to find it yourself," Kathan said while adding:

"What I can do is make your time in the mountains memorable and make this day mean something."

He got up and took Anvi's hand, asking her for a dance, but the old fool didn't even know how to do that properly.

"I do have the confidence to ask you for a dance, but I don't actually know how to," Kathan said while taking out a cigarette.

"No worries; all you have to do is bring your step to the front while I take it back, and vice versa. It's that simple!" Anvi said while taking the cigarette out of his hands and putting it on the table.

"Don't smoke so much, dummy!" Anvi said.

The music complimented their moods, and soon they forgot to focus on the dance as Kathan hugged Anvi, wondering if this is where his pain ends.

"No, it doesn't," said the inner voice. "Pain never ends because of a person; it always ends with you!"

Kathan ignored what the voice said and continued to enjoy the dance while embracing Anvi's warm affection.

He continued to push Anvi's hair beyond her ears, but they would always come back, giving him another chance to touch those loose tresses that whispered tales of warmth and vulnerability in his ears.

Kathan lost himself in the fruity smell of those strands of hair and wondered if he could freeze that moment and live it over and over again.

His breath fell on Anvi's neck as he whispered something in her ears. She felt herself losing composure and was helpless to work against it. Kathan realized how Anvi's body was a work of art that he needed to worship.

Kathan's beating heart merged with Anvi's, and the two embraced each other like fallen angels, meeting after an eternity. Goosebumps were felt by both as his face was submerged in her eyes.

"Wait a minute!" Anvi said while moving towards the table and fixing herself another drink.

Kathan, who was already under the influence of warm feelings, blurry visions, and booze, drank straight from the bottle.

"I don't know if I've told you this, but sometimes I wish I could freeze time. I always know that the things that I want the most in life are placed here, right on the palm of my hands, only to be snatched from me when I try to close my wrist," Kathan said.

"You're going to feel pretty bad when I leave, won't you?" Anvi said. "Yes, you would!"

"Well, you did say you had two days here," Kathan replied. "But then, who has seen tomorrow? Maybe this is it."

Kathan held Anvi's dinky face in his warm palms, proceeded to kiss her on the forehead, and then looked into her shining eyes. Thereafter, he kissed her left cheek and, once again, looked her in the eye, finally kissing her on the lips.

The two had finally embraced the moment, but all of a sudden, Anvi pushed Kathan away, asking him to accompany her to the dorm.

Kathan was confused but did as he was asked. Anvi wasn't able to walk properly, possibly due to intoxication and aching legs after roaming the entire city. Writer *Sahab* carried her in his arms for a short distance.

"You're an asshole, you know that?" Kathan's inner voice said.

Apurva was waiting for Anvi with an irritated face.

"Guess what?" Apurva asked.

"What?" Kathan and Anvi simultaneously said.

"Well, there's this guy Shivam who's been on my social media and wants to know if you're with me," Apurva said.

Anvi's face tourned sour.

"There's a real world out there; social media is a mess," Kathan suggested.

Kathan took Anvi's hand and turned her around to face him.

"Are you upset with me?" Kathan asked.

"I'm going to answer you tomorrow. I think you should sleep for now, and I need to attend to some shit that Apurva has done," Anvi said.

"Got it," Kathan patiently said, sitting on his bed.

A few minutes later, Kathan once again got up and walked towards Anvi while taking out his wallet.

"Here!" Kathan said.

"What's this?" Anvi questioned.

"This is a lucky coin that I believe works. I hope you sort out whatever fucked-up situation you're dealing with," Kathan said while handing the coin to Anvi.

"Thank you so much," Anvi said while hugging Kathan once again and asking him to go to bed.

Apurva and Anvi were engaged in a heavy discussion through whispers, and it seemed to revolve around this person named Shivam.

Once again, Kathan crept up on the two of them and asked Apurva to come towards him, handing her a piece of paper.

"Give Anvi this paper when she is at her lowest," Kathan silently said in Apurva's ear.

"What was that about?" Anvi questioned.

"Nothing. He just wanted to say goodnight," Apurva said.

Kathan gradually fell asleep while Apurva and Anvi continued their discussion.

The two girls continued their conversation, and an hour passed by. A few minutes later, they decided to pack their bags and leave the hostel for reasons known only to them.

Apurva led the way, opening the door, while Anvi followed behind, looking at Kathan with her bright innocent eyes and leaving a kiss on his forehead.

"He does look cute while sleeping," Apurva said.

"Fuck off! Remind me, I have to answer his question in a text," Anvi said.

The two left the dorm.

"Tender hearts and warm embraces,

Broken souls and pretty faces.

We all have our weaknesses; we all seek happiness through love,

We are all kids at heart; some hide it well enough.

The forbidden kiss—did it mean something?

If not, it will definitely sting.

Broken hearts can only understand each other,

Feelings can create a pother.

A shield was created to protect the heart,

A sword was created to perfect the art.

Of falling for a person at first sight,

Knowing that with them, there won't be a second night."

CHAPTER TEN

GOODBYES

Kathan woke up from his deep slumber, and as soon as his eyes opened, he looked at the bed occupied by Anvi, only to find that it had been vacated and someone else was waiting for it to be cleaned out so they could claim the bed.

"What the hell?" Kathan exclaimed.

He ran towards the front desk to inquire about Anvi and Apurva's whereabouts.

"Sir, they both checked out at around 3 AM," the manager said.

Kathan couldn't comprehend this situation, and somewhere he felt like it was all his fault.

He thought of calling Anvi but remembered that she had his number, but he didn't.

"It's quite fucked up, isn't it?" Kathan's inner voice said while ridiculing him.

He hurriedly went back to his room to find his phone, which was discharged.

"Where the fuck is my charger?" Kathan cursed while others around him started looking at him in a strange way.

He took out his charger from his bag and finally got the phone switched on. He waited for a few minutes and then took the phone out of charge, holding it in his hands, and walked towards the stream.

Johnny was seated in his usual position, and Kathan sat beside him. Manny was nowhere to be seen.

Kathan opened the message application and was relieved to find a message from Anvi, which read:

"And I wasn't mad at you. It was just that you kissed me, and I felt kind of sad because we might not see each other anytime soon. Last night was special and will always mean something for me. I will call you once I've sorted out my mess. Don't forget me, writer Sahab."

Kathan was delighted, and his mood was uplifted. On the other hand, Johnny thought this to be a signal of play time and immediately jumped, placing his front paws on Kathan's chest, making him lose balance.

While Kathan was able to save himself from falling into the stream, his phone slid from his hand, falling into the water body. He watched as the current carried away his phone from him, ending his only source of contact with Anvi.

He felt dejected, shattered, and bruised, and an unbearable pain strangled his heart. At that moment, Kathan gave up.

"I guess you don't have any choice but to listen to me now. Let's go back to our doomed apartment, devoid of any independence, and stare at the wall," the inner voice said as Kathan went back into the dorm, packed his bags, and left for his apartment in the city.

***

"Did Kathan reply to your message?" Apurva asked.

"No! Do you think he's mad that we left without telling him?" Anvi said.

"I don't know. He's your type; you should know better. I'm not drawn towards people who are fucked up," Apurva said.

"Maybe I should call him?" Anvi was questioned while dialing his number.

"Damn, it's not reachable," she said.

"If it's of any use, I'm so sorry. I didn't know that Shivam was your cousin! He saw the status update on my social media and asked if you were with me. I had put our picture in the city with the location," Apurva said.

"Well, it is possible that they might now come after me. So, it's better if we just bail. How many days of our leave are left?" Anvi questioned.

"Um, we still have around three days, including today. Let's go to that place we had planned," Apurva said.

"Miss Apurva, could you remind us why we didn't invite Kathan with us?" Anvi asked.

"It didn't cross my mind, you know. Now that I think about it, he could've tagged along and held our bags for us. Don't you think he had strong arms, huh?" Apurva said while teasing Anvi.

"Shut up, or I'll throw you off the cliff," Anvi replied.

"Dear passengers," said the taxi driver. "If you need to stuff your stomachs, do it now because I'm not going to stop for the next two hours, and that is the approximate time it will take to reach the destination."

Anvi, Apurva, and the others started getting out of the vehicle.

"For the people getting out of the other side, please watch out for oncoming vehicles, or you'll have to pay for the doors," said the driver while laughing and ordering a tea for himself.

"Cigarette?" Apurva asked.

"Sure!"

The two girls were once again smoking the cancer stick, while Anvi's mind was occupied by the thoughts of the person she left in the hostel.

"Would you like to hear a story in exchange for 5 paise?" The old sage once again appeared out of nowhere.

Anvi and Apurva were stunned by his sudden appearance and this time, offered a five hundred rupee note to the sage.

"Huh, do you think I care for this lowly stuff? I am one of the Nagas; I live in the holy land and only meet people in need of a hand," the sage said.

"Don't you feel cold? At least cover your essentials," Apurva said.

"Offer me a cup of tea, and I'll tell you a story. All you have to do is give me 5 paise," the sage replied.

"How on earth will I find a coin worth 5 paise?" Anvi questioned.

"That's your headache," the sage replied.

"Firstly, here's your tea," Apurva said.

"Sit down, have your cigarette, and I'll have my *bidi*. If you want, you can try a *bidi* as well. However, I doubt you'll like it," the sage said.

"No please!" Anvi and Apurva spoke simultaneously as the old sage laughed.

"I'm old, and I've seen a lot of things in my life. Today, I'll tell you the story of a man who talks to himself," the sage said. "This man lives in an apartment, all alone, and one fine day, he finally breaks down. He took drugs, smoked cigarettes, and laid with women, but nothing worked because, at the end of the day, the voice in his head controlled his actions."

"So what? We all have our inner monologue; that doesn't make this guy any special," Apurva interrupted.

"Well, one fine day, he decided to go on a murderous spree and ended up getting stuck in a struggle between the good and the bad. The two people that meant the most to him in that moment were killed in front of him, and all he could do was sit and do nothing. When he got the opportunity, he ran. He ran from everything to a far-off place, searching for the meaning of his miserable life. For a few days, he thought he had succeeded in finding the purpose of life, but he couldn't have been more wrong," the sage continued.

"Why the hell are you telling this story to us?" Anvi questioned.

"Who knows? I've been sent here to tell this story to you, and so I'm telling it. At the end of the day, the man concluded that he had failed his life, failed his purpose, failed his loved ones, and that there was no way out of this adorable mess we all call life. He ends his life by coming underneath a large vehicle. Maybe, in his mind, he always knew that the end was destined, but facing it was an impossible task for him. My ladies, hope is something that can bring back the dead, but it is also something that can hollow a man from the inside. Too many attempts at securing victory make the win worthless," the sage said while ending his story.

"So, do you have my five paise?" The sage asks once again.

"No, we don't! Please stop troubling us!" Anvi and Apurva said.

"Find me when you have the coin, because his peace lies with you," the sage said while pointing his index finger at Anvi and once again returning to the path he came from.

"Whose peace?" Anvi questioned.

"This man is a complete idiot. He has been roaming the mountains since I was a young kid, and hell, now I have my own three kids, and his bullshit does not stop. He is drunk all the time; don't mind him," the driver said, while the tea shop owner agreed.

"He is a regular. He always troubles customers, and they give him some money to drive him away," the shop owner added.

"But he didn't take our money. He just wants 5 paise," Anvi said.

"Might be high or drunk at the moment," the driver said.

"Don't fall for the words of such idiots," the driver added. "Well, I'm going to give you all a few more minutes, freshen up, and then we'll leave."

***

"Anvi, there is this middle-aged woman that has been eyeing us constantly. Should I ask what her problem is?" Apurva said.

"Go ahead," Anvi said while finishing up her cigarette.

"*Namaste!* I couldn't help but notice that you've been looking at us since we stopped here. Is there any problem?" Apurva said it in a not-so-polite manner.

"Oh, you noticed! Don't bother. You two look like my daughters. They are currently studying abroad, and my husband and I came to the mountains to enjoy the time we have left on this earth," the woman said.

"Sorry if I came out as rude," Apurva said.

"Well, this is how the times have evolved. I love women who have the courage to speak to another person like this. Back in my young days, we didn't have the bravery and authority to speak to a man, especially our father, in an authoritative way. I remember when I was young, whenever my father called out my name, I would feel so scared," the woman said.

"Damn, you cool *auntyji*," Anvi said.

"Well, what's your name?" The woman asked Apurva.

"Apurva," she said.

"Your face looks quite similar to mine when I was young. Where are you from?" The woman asked.

"We came from the city," Apurva said. "We work at an architecture firm as interns."

"Nice," the woman said.

"So, are you returning home?" The woman asked.

"No, we are going to another hill station, around two hours away. I guess you'll exit the journey somewhere in between." Apurva noted.

"Yes!" The woman said.

"I feel that the two of you are going through something. May I be of any help?" The woman asked.

"Well, there's family stuff. This lady here has a pretty messed-up family. They're trying to get her married and whatnot," Apurva said while pointing at her friend.

"You know what? Fuck the family! Come in here; I'll give you a little secret. See, these ten years of your life are very critical—the world awaits you. Take advantage of that glowing skin and that beautiful health and climb mountains, cross rivers, and do anything you feel like. Don't complicate your life with postponing decisions or making strong shields—you won't end up anywhere," the woman said.

"When I was young, I wanted to be so many things, and among them was a painter. Then I got married, only to be the mother of two daughters. It's not like I don't love my daughters, but I just hate the fact that I wasn't ever able to discover what I could've been. The time is gone now. There's just one shot we all get at life," added the woman.

"It is not that easy!" Anvi said. "There are situations, their consequences, and so much more that only I know!"

"See, you have to live in the present from your heart and think about the future from your mind. If you do it the wrong way, you'll always be anxious about the future and fuck up your present. Learn to give everything a chance in life, travel more, and dream more, and you might fall down in the process. If your family fails to pick you up and you have to lick your wounds alone, abandon them!"

"Hm," Anvi said.

"Here's a little poem I wrote back when I got to know that I'd get married and wouldn't be able to paint anymore," the woman said.

"They say,

If you're happy, you cannot create art:

You'll need to go through the same painful experience from the start.

Indulge me for a moment,

Life is a wave of happiness, boredom, and sadness:

This trifecta in life is possibly endless.

What could possibly go wrong,

We have limited time here:

Why not spend it in good faith and without fear.

You see,

It's not necessary to leave everything—the comfort, the stability—to achieve greatness,

It's futile, overrated how people define success.

Without art,

Yes, we would never exist:

But you see, art is only valuable in the eyes of another broken heart.

Who cares how much time you spent drawing the portrait or writing the perfect story?

People are selfish; they will just single out your shortcomings, pointless and gory."

***

The driver started honking, and the conversation between the two girls and the woman ended abruptly. People started hurriedly getting in the taxi, and it was time to leave Mussoorie and drive towards the other hill station.

"People say that we can see snow-covered mountains from that place," Apurva cheerfully said while receiving no reply from Anvi.

"What happened?" Apurva questioned.

"Nothing; I was just thinking about the stuff that the lady said," Anvi replied.

"Well, she definitely got in your mind and mine too!" Apurva said. "That's the reason I have now decided: I will live in the present and sometimes think about the future. I would suggest you do the same."

"Yep, you're right!" Anvi said.

The vehicle started moving, following curved roads that seemed to end at a point, but a single turn would give birth to a multitude of others. The lush green leaves encapsulated in the cold and fresh air gave the mind a peaceful resolution from struggles.

"A fun fact about the mountains," said the driver. "You will find that many men here are intoxicated almost throughout the day. You won't even know that they are drunk. Well, since the population density between the city and the hill stations differs greatly, your places have more sponges, but nevertheless, even tourists here come only to drink during the weekends."

"You're not drunk, right?" A man in the back asked.

"I used to be! But then, a year ago, I was too drunk to drive, and as a result, I got into an accident, and one of the passengers died. Luckily, it was an old woman, and the others were quite young, so they survived. Since then, I haven't touched liquor, and I'm still trying to pay off the family of the old woman," the driver added.

A few minutes passed, and one by one, the passengers started leaving the taxi as they each reached their destiny. It was time for the old woman to leave as well.

"Anvi, Apurva, it was nice meeting you both. If I must say one last thing, don't try to win life; it's not a competition. Experience it, change your palate, meet new people, fall in love, fall out of love—you only have limited time. God knows, I have cancer, and I might not live so long, but take this suggestion from me—fuck everyone and just live," said the woman as her husband helped her out of the car and towards their destination.

CHAPTER ELEVEN

A STRANGE MAN

Anvi and Apurva had two more days before they left for the city, their minds uncaring and uncertain of what awaited them.

"Well, I know I won't get into any trouble. Your fucked-up life only belongs to you, love; I have enough on my plate," Apurva said while standing on the balcony of their new hotel's room.

"Whatever! This new place is awesome, though," Anvi replied.

"I know!" Apurva agreed. "Look at those snow-capped mountains far away. It's like they are on the same level as us and look so calm and peaceful. You know, when I woke up in the morning, I saw three children from a nearby village, accompanied by a dog and a herd of sheep. They were saying that this place also experiences snowfall during peak winters. We should definitely come back soon!"

"Yeah, if I'm not married to a moron by then," Anvi replied.

"Don't be so negative. Just change your place, and no one will be able to find you. At most, they'd be looking for you in Mussoorie, but we're quite far from that place," Apurva suggested. "Just chill, and here, have this beer."

Anvi took the bottle and opened the cap with her teeth, giggling.

"What are you laughing about all of a sudden?" Apurva asked.

"Well, I remembered a story a cousin of mine used to say. There was his friend who once tried opening a beer bottle's cap with one of his teeth, and it came off! Every time since then, I fear what if I lost one of my prized teeth while opening this bottle," Anvi said.

Apurva started laughing as well. The stress that the two had been carrying vanished for a moment in the giggles of someone's stupidity, a story which may or may not be true.

"It's just so beautiful," Anvi said while looking at the clouds making irregular patterns with birds chirping in different voices and beautiful dogs following tourists that they had just met.

"It's strange how once we start focusing on the positives of life, we let go of all the deep and smelly shit we are in," Anvi said.

The sun was shining brightly, and every few minutes, a vehicle would pass by, echoing through the mountains.

"There is no noise up here, just you and your thoughts, and maybe this is what life is supposed to be all about," Anvi continued.

"Okay, Miss Philosopher! Let me let you in on a secret. Now that I know you like writers, there is one leaving this place today. Why don't you go and talk to him?" Apurva said.

"I'm done with writers. The one I met hasn't texted or called me back, and his number is not reachable. I don't like being ghosted, and that is the last time I'm letting a guy do this to me," Anvi said.

"Well, there is no harm in talking," Apurva said. "Let's go; I'm getting bored."

The duo went downstairs in search of the writer, who was supposed to be leaving the place after finishing up his new work.

"I came to know that a certain writer is also here," Apurva asked at the reception.

"Yeah, he's a regular. Sometimes, it seems like he lives in the mountains, like he's one of us now," the man said. "There he is, packing his stuff on his bike."

Anvi and Apurva went outside, finding the writer.

"Hello! I'm Apurva, and she's Anvi. We heard you write." Apurva questioned.

"Yeah, I just completed my second book, and now I'm off to the city. There's a lot of work involved. I need to get it published and everything," the writer said. "By the way, my name is Parth."

"Oh, you're the one that Kathan talked about back in Mussoorie," Anvi said.

"Kathan? Oh yeah, I met him. He kind of reminded me of my old self," Parth said.

"Yeah, well, he's okay," Anvi said.

"Haha! You know, the first time I came to the mountains, I was told that whatever you seek to achieve here, you will attract faster amid these peaks. Since then, whenever I come back, I get one story after another—it's like they just walk towards me," Parth said.

"That's cool," Anvi replied.

"Maybe you two might find answers to some of your troubles too; just keep your ears, eyes, and hearts open!" Parth said while getting on his bike.

"It was nice meeting you," Apurva said.

"Same. Here, take this," Parth said while handing Anvi his first book. "Read it and let me know if you like it."

"How will I let you know?" Anvi questioned.

"If you truly like it, you will find ways to let me know," Parth said while starting his bike and riding away.

"Damn, writers are strange people," Apurva said.

"I know, right? Everything is a damn story for them," Anvi said.

***

Anvi and Apurva were outside of their hotel, soaking in the beautiful atmosphere at 7,500 feet above sea level. The freezing temperature, coupled with the clean air and the warmth provided by the sun overhead would heal any broken soul in an instant.

"Hey Anvi, look at that person. It seems like he's crying," Apurva said.

From the corner of the road emerged a man wearing a torn jacket, baggy pants, a T-shirt on the inside, and dirty boots. He had a red scarf around his neck that had turned brown due to the dirt that had accumulated on it during the course of his life's journey in the past few days.

Indeed, tears had been running down his cheeks, and contrary to what others might say, a crying man looks like a tiger that has been run over by a jeep housed by tourists who were interested in exploring the jungle—feeble, worthless, and of no use.

It was a poor sight, and everyone on the outside was rapidly retracing their steps inside their four walls, reducing the chances of unnecessary exposure. No one wanted to mingle with this man or ask the reason for his sadness.

On the other hand, Anvi and Apurva were also advised by the man at the reception to come inside and pay no heed to the man, who was obviously drunk and mourning the loss of someone who meant a lot to him.

Out of the blue, the man took out a few photographs from his coat's pocket and started tearing the pictures, throwing the pieces in the air as they rained heavily back on earth.

Any activity done with enough emotions seems reasonable to the person doing it and indeed, bottling up emotions is a fucked-up thing to do.

"Should we ask this person what happened?" Apurva asked Anvi.

"A big no from my side," Anvi said.

"Well, let's have a look at the pictures that he has torn," Apurva advised.

The man passed by Apurva and Anvi, paying no heed to their existence but just throwing away the photographs that he kept close to his heart.

Apurva hurriedly went towards the place where she first saw the man and noticed that he had been walking for quite some time, leaving bits and pieces of pictures throughout the road. She picked up a few pieces and tried to put them together, an event that birthed the face of a girl.

"This is a picture of a girl in a marriage saree. It seems to be his wife, or maybe his lover?" Apurva said.

Anvi joined Apurva in the hunt for the pieces, and as they put together the photos, the two realized that the photos were clicked of the man and the woman, who was supposedly his wife, when they stood side-by-side at their marriage ceremony.

"Quite a twisted story we have on our hands," Anvi said.

"It seems odd! Look how he has changed. The man in the photos and the man going in front of us are the same and yet so different—it makes me wonder. At any moment,

I might lose everything and become worthless in the eyes of others," Apurva commented.

"C'mon, there's no need to be so sentimental. He might've done something that pushed the girl away, and she might've run away with someone with more money or possibly more resources," Anvi said.

As the man continued to walk, the people who were ignoring him earlier gradually came together to gossip about the person behind his back. However, the man didn't care and kept walking, sobbing over his loss and wondering what he could do to bring the girl he lost back into her life.

Everyone was busy collecting whatever photos they could so they could put together a picture of what had happened.

"It seems that her wife ran away with someone. I had heard something related to this a few days ago," a woman said.

"I think she married him to satisfy her family and then eloped with a lover of hers from the city. Women nowadays have no shame," another woman added.

"Don't be so quick to judge, ladies," a man chimed in from the back.

"Things can be quite different from the inside. Don't base your stories off of rumors," added the man at the reception.

"It could be anything," the other man continued.

When the crowd started dispersing, a car came in filled with two men, who got out and started asking questions.

"Have you seen a man walking around here in shabby clothes, crying?" The driver asked.

The other man also asked similar questions of others. No one was interested in answering the questions asked by the two men until they arrived at Anvi and Apurva.

"Yeah, we saw the man. He was crying and tearing a few photographs of possibly her wife. He went straight ahead. You might get him; he couldn't have gotten far away," Apurva said.

"Go, catch him," the other man asked the driver, who obeyed.

"If you don't mind me asking, what is the story behind this person?" Anvi questioned.

"Well, long story short, he was married almost a year ago, and his wife died while giving birth to his only son. Just a few hours after birth, the son also gave up on life, and now he's left alone. His family wants him to remarry, but he doesn't want to do so because he still cares about his wife. What a strange time we're living in! There are loads of facilities in the cities, but no one cares about the mountains," said the man.

"There are not enough people here, so they don't care about us. The people with houses on the roads are still better than those who are living in the villages," said a woman who was eavesdropping on the conversation.

"What can we do? I was supposed to be retired, but the other officers were caught up, so I was asked by this man's family to catch him and bring him back," said the man.

Moments later, the driver was seen holding the man's collar and dragging his drunk self towards the car.

"I don't want to go," said the drunkard while crying his eyes out. "I lost her; I lost my blood; what's more for me?"

"If my father loved me and my mother this much, life would've been so much better," Anvi whispered in Apurva's ear.

"Men seem complicated to me. They don't know how to express themselves, but when they do, they destroy their reputation," Apurva added.

The drunk man freed himself from the clutches of the driver and tried running away, only to be caught by the other man that arrived in the vehicle with him.

"Listen to me," said the man while slurring his words.

"Go on," said the man while holding his collar.

"Take me to those girls," said the drunkard.

"Nope," the man replied.

"I'll go with you, I promise," said the hopeless man.

"Okay," his captivator replied.

"I'd like to ask you both something," the man said.

"Sure," Anvi and Apurva said.

"If you lose someone that you hold in high regard, what do you do? How do you move on? Should I just give up and move on? How do I honor the memory of the person that I loved? Now, don't tell me that bullshit that I loved the idea of that person or that I'm in love with those memories we shared. What we had was real, and you both are too young to understand that philosophies do not work in real life; their ideal place remains in the mind. You can't rationalize actions with philosophies, is what I'm trying to say. So, answer me," the man said while falling to the ground, once again sobbing.

The two girls were dumbfounded, for they did not know the answer to the question that they were still trying to unravel. The questions took Anvi's world by storm, and she started questioning her decision to run away from her home and not stay with her family through these tough times when they might be feeling what the drunk man in front of her was feeling.

However, she was quick enough to recover from these thoughts of self-doubt and decided to stick with what she had decided.

"Is it even worth it?" Anvi said. "The memories that are eating you alive are the shadows imprinted on your mind of a person who has left this realm. If they are gone, the relationship between the two of you doesn't exist anymore, and what doesn't exist anymore does not have a future or a past; it is merely a memory that only you will remember. With age, you will also forget. It hurts now because it's fresh, but it won't be five years from now," Anvi said while walking away towards a tea shop nearby.

Soon the drunk man was taken by the men that had arrived in their vehicles, and the crowd dispersed. Minutes later, everything was back to normal; some were reading their newspapers, some were listening to the radio, while others were engaged in their daily chores, getting ready for the holiday season, where tourists enter the place like an army trying to conquer an already unstable fort.

Anvi and Apurva decided to smoke cigarettes, and it was the first time that they were not sharing. The man's existence had shaken their souls, and as many have said, looking at life too closely might make you not live it.

"Anvi, what's the plan for tomorrow?" Apurva asked while breaking the silence that lasted for a few minutes.

"Well, let's go to that viewpoint that everyone is talking about. It is said that during the sunset, everything turns orange, and I'd love to see that," Anvi replied.

"Sure!" Apurva agreed.

"Doesn't this poem perfectly summarize the situation of the man that you just saw?" The old sage once again returned, this time wearing an orange cloth around his groin and a huge turban on his head.

"If twenty people trouble me right now,
And ask me to change, I won't be able to figure out how.
For sure, ladies, my soul is lost,

But, I repeat again, I can't pay the cost.
The problem is, I want to give up,
I want to empty my cup:
That holds so many thoughts.
It's not like I'm suffering from some disease,
I've seen too much of life, and I just can't release:
The pent-up frustration that the eye sees.
It's like cigarette burns that sting,
Such painful songs that I forget to sing.
I think I'm being evil,
All my thoughts are medieval.
It doesn't make sense now; nothing does,
Am I suicidal? Will I ever be happy?
Why am I always filled with anger and regret?
I have faced so many losses,
I don't know the path that my heart crosses.
Love is not the answer to anything, nor is moving on,
Self-satisfaction isn't the key, and peace is momentary.
Life is fucked up,
I'm unable to empty my cup.
My array of thoughts have destroyed me,
Escapance is my reality.
I am sorry to all those who ever put their faith in me,
That's what I have been trying to tell you for the past few
days,
I'm insane, and this is the story of my insanity.

CHAPTER TWELVE

WHERE ENDS MEET

"Once again, you're here. How do you do that?" Anvi asked.

"I don't know. You two tell me," the sage said.

"I don't have a damn five-paise coin," Anvi replied.

"Me too," Apurva agreed.

"Where in this day and age will you find a five-paise coin? Are you drunk or just high?" An angry Anvi questioned.

"I am a sage; I have no need to be intoxicated, for I am always drunk on nature and on the things that surround you," the sage said.

"Well, this time you did have the decency to wear proper clothes," said Apurva.

"That is because this will be the last time I beg you for the coin," the sage said. "Haven't you learned anything on this journey? Everything is connected; it's all a puzzle. The Creator does not do anything without reason," the sage noted.

"I have learned a few things. First of all, everyone needs to be happy because they deserve to be so. The poem you recited above implies that he was a drunk, sad man because he chose to be so. I can be sad about my father's death too, but I choose not to be, for there is nothing I can do that will bring him back and answer my questions. What is the point?" Anvi said.

"That, my lady, is true," the sage said. "But you are forgetting something. Those who are gone have their regrets; they take their remorse with them, and when reborn, they have a sense of guilt that constantly tells them that they do not deserve what they receive in the next life."

"So? According to your logic, there is a 100 percent chance that my father will be reborn and that he will live a horrible life, thinking that he did something wrong. That doesn't benefit me in either way," Anvi argued. "There is no point to anything. We all just attach meaning to bullshit via philosophy."

"If what you're saying is true, then maybe there is no need for the coin to exchange hands. You are still in need of a lot of luck," the sage said.

"What the hell does that mean?" Anvi asked.

"It doesn't matter, as you said," the sage replied.

"Oh sir, welcome back!" Exclaimed the manager of the hotel where Anvi and Apurva were staying. "Come in, have some tea."

"No, maybe some other time," the sage said. "I feel that, currently, I'm not welcome here. I can't step into places where forgiveness fails to create a home for itself."

"Please stop talking in riddles," an irritated Anvi said.

"Ma'am, you're disrespecting a Naga. He has seen enough, heard everything, and learned about most of the things that we cannot fathom," the manager said.

"Maybe. But all I see is a man who has gone senile with age," Anvi replied while walking back into the room.

"I apologize on her behalf. She is just a little troubled with all the shit that she has seen through the days. Additionally, a man she likes has ghosted her so she can be like that," Apurva said.

"There is a man for every girl, and every man has a path that leads to a girl. It is all a circle, and we are all planets, revolving in a meaningless orbit in search of momentary happiness," the sage said.

The sage left after drinking the water that the manager gave him, while Apurva left to be at her friend's side, who was going through some complex emotions.

***

"You didn't have to be so mean to the sage," Apurva said.

"I'm tired of this old dude creeping up to us every time asking for something that we don't have," Anvi said.

"Well, here's something that might cheer up your mood," Apurva replied.

"What?" Anvi questioned.

"Um, I know I can't solve your complex problems, but what I can do is give you this paper that Kathan handed over to me before we left. He asked me to give this to you when you are feeling the most horrible," Apurva said.

Anvi took the piece of paper hastily and immediately started reading it.

"We sat across from each other, perplexed,
Her eyes shone brightly with joy that was vexed:
It was in the moment that, under the burden of emotions,
my shoulders flexed.
Eyes are the closest relatives to any soul, any emotion,
After all, we are what our memories make us:
Our decisions guide our ship through the ocean.
I was under a lot of pressure, or maybe a little confused,
Was this the moment I replayed over and over?

Was this the change I was seeking since I don't know, like forever?

The deeper your thoughts, the wider your eyes,

The clearer your conscience, the more confidence in it subsides:

The happier you are, the more satisfaction there lies.

It's all in the moment you look at someone,

Their glory, their worries, their lust, and their complexity are all undone:

A weathered soul resides somewhere in there,

I guess away from the world, in her eyes, her true emotions had come.

Those beautiful little curvatures, like shadowed little soldiers,

Asked me to console them and lift off the heavy boulders:

Of regret, pain, and anxiety, was she carrying the same weight on her shoulders?

She wanted to utter the words, but the world held her back, creating doubt,

This world is an evil place, and it's the demons in it that we are better without:

I want to know what we are both scared about,

Is it mine or her 'previous self' that is standing right out?

I feel like I've been quiet for so long. I'm cold and numb,

In a nutshell, my tongue has dried up like cracks on the road:

I feel I am poisonous to everyone around me, as if I were a toad.

I think it would have been easier if the Future or Lady Luck were sitting beside us,

If our guardian Angels were not stuck in their own blood-stained corrupt sins:

I just want this to be a little easier than the nights I've been drunk, trudging through the dustbins.

Right in front of me, she was sitting. I was just clueless,

Then, I just looked into her eyes, and suddenly everything faded out of my sight:

As if the whole place were swallowed by night itself and the only light–

Was coming from her face, I felt helpless.

Her eyelashes, as if the keys to a piano, sang me such a heavenly tune,

The tune that only my eyes could decipher, and suddenly, in the winter, I felt as the weather turned into early June.

It's just an organ, just a couple of circles; I tried to wake my mind up,

My heart had shut itself off, advising me to just keep up.

What had her eyes done to me?

Why suddenly did all my dreams make me weak like a beaten, bruised, and hollowed tree?

Her intentions seemed so clear and free.

Suddenly my heart said, "Go tell her idiot, you are falling for her innocence."

It was weird; how could someone still be innocent in this world full of pestilence?

I was unable to figure this out,

Then she asked me, "Are you still in doubt?"

I was unable to speak; my skin was vomiting water,

I was wondering if my anger and doubt were the cousins of Fear's daughter.

I had a feeling deep down that I wasn't floating; my heart was just above the water.

It has been so long since I longed for someone like this,

It has been so long since I wasn't wronged by someone like this:

I guess it's just those innocent eyes that make me think like this.

You see, I woke myself up and stopped creating this fairy tale,

There's no innocence; every emotion I have manifested will soon turn into an ail.

Everyone seems to be human, but, since the beginning of time, we have all had a tail.

These eyes are a drug; don't give in to them anymore,

You will get high, and then your skull will be bashed into the floor.

This little work of mine is just a manifestation of a weird soul:

Well, even though it's been chewed up and spit out whole,

Still, somewhere, it believes in the magic of those eyes,

It's tragic; it's lies:

For you, my heart still tries."

Anvi read the entire poem and broke down, sobbing herself to sleep. Soon, Apurva also joined her friend, and the two fell into a deep slumber.

***

"So, this is the final day of the trip. Let's go to the place we talked about," Apurva said. "A taxi is waiting for us outside; hurry!"

Anvi didn't bother changing clothes because she was still feeling horrible. Her muscles put in more effort than a man does to cut down a tree, and she pushed her body off the bed.

"Let's go," Anvi said.

The two traveled to a place where the locals said tourists stopped to only see the sun set. Not many people were present at the location, and there was a single tea shop where an old lady and a man were trying their hardest to satisfy the never-ending demands of their customers.

Anvi and Apurva got off the vehicle that would wait for them for almost half an hour. The sun was losing its power to the night, and an orange tint covered the sky. The clouds also lost their white shade, and the sky started turning purple, with the moon gradually embracing its responsibility.

The brightest stars in the sky were coming out of their hiding places, and with each second passing, the mountains went more and more quiet.

"It feels so good," Anvi said. "Look at everything. It just paints a calm picture in your heart, doesn't it?"

"Yes, it does," Apurva said while immediately capturing the scene on her phone.

Meanwhile, Anvi decided to savor the moment with tea and *pakoras*, a delicacy for which the old couple has been famous for years.

"Hello, Uncle, can we get two plates of *pakoras*?" Anvi asked.

"Sure, child," the old man replied while asking her wife to make some.

"How long have you two been here?" Anvi questioned.

"I forgot the count soon after I was married to this girl," said the old man.

"So, was it a love marriage, or did your parents arrange it for you?" Anvi asked.

"Well, our parents knew each other, and we kind of knew that we were meant to be together the first time we saw each other in person," the old man said. "You'll understand this feeling once you get to that level of maturity."

"I was feeling quite irritated and lashed out on a sage yesterday, but coming here, I'm at peace, and now I feel I shouldn't have behaved the way I did," Anvi said.

"If you're talking about the Naga that roams these mountains, he's been here for years, preaching forgiveness. We all hold him in high regard," said the old man. "Many people have disrespected him for his views on life; he's probably used to it."

"I guess you're right," Anvi continued.

"Here's your tea and pakoras," the old lady said while coming out of the kitchen. "Sit down here; you'll get the perfect view."

"You know what? The sage kept asking me for a five-paise coin, and I kept telling him that I didn't have any," Anvi told the old man and the lady.

"Maybe you do have it," the old lady said. "Check it."

Anvi decided to open her wallet and start going through it. She found money, chewing gum, and some hair clips, and turned the wallet upside down as a few coins fell to the ground.

Surprised, Anvi picked up these coins, going through each one, but all were either one or two rupee coins except the one that fell further away from her.

She picked up that one coin and was astonished to see that it was a five-paise coin.

"Where did this come from?" Anvi questioned.

"Maybe someone gave it to you on the way," the old man said.

Anvi tried to recall but couldn't figure out how she got the five-paise coin.

"Didn't Kathan give you something before you hugged him on the night we left? Something he described as his 'lucky charm'?" Apurva said.

"Oh shit," Anvi exclaimed.

"Where can I find this sage?" Anvi asked the old man.

"He comes and goes as he pleases. He might come right out of that corner, hitchhiking," replied the old man.

Dejected, Anvi sat down. She knew it was her last day in the mountains, and a certain guilt was eating away at her.

"Eat the pakoras, or they'll turn cold," the old lady said.

Anvi and Apurva started eating the delicacy, and once again, the sound of motorcycle exhausts echoing through the mountains was heard.

"Oh my God, I'm going to kill these bikers. They think they're the king of mountains or something. Every time they have to announce that they are coming via their loud machines," Apurva said.

The motorcyclists, on their bikes, passed by, each person waving to the old lady and her husband as if they knew them personally. When the last motorbiker emerged from the corner, Anvi and Apurva saw the old sage, seated in a distinct and unconventional manner, as a pillion, facing the opposite direction from the rider.

The sage laughed and waved towards Anvi and Apurva, positioned with his front side turned toward the rear of the motorcycle, saying goodbye while the two tried to call him and ask him to stop.

"What the hell?" Anvi cursed the situation. "He didn't stop!"

The two paid the shop owners and left for the hotel, eventually returning to the city the next day.

***

A number of weeks had passed since Anvi and Apurva went to the mountains, and after returning, the two immediately shifted their stuff to a new place.

"Anvi, won't you ever talk to your mother?" Apurva asked.

119

"I will, but not right now. I need to figure out my shit first," Anvi replied.

"Well, as you wish. Let's go for a cigarette break. I've been cooped up in this apartment for too long," Apurva said.

"Sure!" Anvi added.

The new apartment had its share of inconsistencies. Independence comes at a cost. The two had barely any time to cook for themselves, and cleaning was a monthly routine.

The walls were freshly painted when the two moved in, but gradually, the low-quality coating gave away, and all that remained were stains of white color on a yellowish wall.

Anvi and Apurva went downstairs, where they found their usual tea seller.

"Welcome, madams," said the seller.

"Give us two cigarettes and two teas," Anvi said.

Meanwhile, a man seated near them was reading the newspaper.

"Look at this headline," the man said.

"An unidentified man in his early twenties commits suicide by coming in front of a bus," the man recited the headline. "If this shit is true, even I can make headlines."

"Didn't the sage tell the story of a man who got killed under a large vehicle?" Anvi said this while taking a look at the newspaper.

"Forget about that old dude girl," Apurva said.

"I don't know; there's something familiar with this headline. I feel like I know this person or that I've met him somewhere," Anvi said while folding the newspaper and smoking her cigarette.

www.ingramcontent.com/pod-product-compliance
Lightning Source LLC
Chambersburg PA
CBHW031737150726
47989CB00006B/2495